island apart

forge books by steven raichlen

Island Apart

island apart

steven raichlen

A TOM DOHERTY ASSOCIATES BOOK

NEW YORK

ISLAND APART

Copyright © 2012 by Steven Raichlen

A Forge Book
Published by Tom Doherty Associates, LLC
175 Fifth Avenue
New York, NY 10010

www.tor-forge.com

Forge® is a registered trademark of Tom Doherty Associates, LLC.

ISBN 978-0-7653-3238-7 (hardcover)
ISBN 978-1-4299-6080-9 (e-book)

First Edition: June 2012

Printed in the United States of America

0 9 8 7 6 5 4 3 2 1

To Barbara

Le vent dans mes voiles

contents

You've got to be a special breed to live here. The type of person that can always find something to do, even when there's nothing to do. If you've got to be told what to do, you'd go out of your cotton-picking mind here.

> —Foster Silva (1918–1981), conservationist and Chappaquiddick resident, as quoted in *Chappaquiddick: That Sometimes Separated But Never Equalled Island*

No man is an island . . . he's a peninsula.

> —John Donne, paraphrased by Jefferson Airplane

island apart

prologue

I n the southeast corner of Massachusetts, six miles off
the coast of Cape Cod, lies the island of Martha's Vineyard.

At the eastern end of Martha's Vineyard lies another, much
smaller island called Chappaquiddick.

The island takes its name from the Wampanoag Indian
words *tchepi-aquidenet*, literally "a place or island apart." At
various points in its history—in the wake of Hurricane
Bob in 1991, for example, or after a powerful nor'easter in
2007—Chappaquiddick has been a true island.

More often than not, however, it has been a peninsula—
connected to the rest of Martha's Vineyard by a long slender
strip of beach called Norton Point.

This is the story of a man who suffered great hurt and
came to the island to find safety, seclusion, and solace. It's

about a woman who lost nearly everything—only to find herself.

This is the story of Claire and the Hermit of Chappaquiddick.

1

the hermit of chappaquiddick

No one knew his name. Everyone called him the Hermit. He had lived on Chappaquiddick Island for as long as most people could remember. Not that anyone could recall precisely when he had arrived. Perhaps he rode in on the tidal wave of summer folk, which swells the population of Martha's Vineyard from fifteen thousand year-round residents to more than a hundred thousand in August.

He certainly didn't look like the typical beachgoer who rode the Chappaquiddick ferry. His wild silvery-gray hair tumbled past his shoulders. A beard as wavy as eelgrass plunged halfway down his chest. The man wore a faded flannel shirt—even in summer—and his jeans had been mended so often, you couldn't make out where the denim ended and the patches began. His feet were clad in lug boots—even in July. As for the color of his eyes, no one could tell, for he always kept them downcast.

The man boarded the ferry as he always did—a few steps behind the other passengers. He placed his ticket on the binnacle rather than handing it directly to the deckhand. His orange ticket identified him as a year-rounder, but no ferry captain could quite recall selling him a commuter book. The tourists gathered at the front of the boat—a pastel swirl of Lilly Pulitzer and Polo—with sunburns that turned pale New England flesh the electric orange of boiled lobsters. The Hermit stood at the stern, his faded clothes blown by the wind, an island unto himself.

If the Hermit had a car, the ferry captains had never seen it. Nor a bicycle or moped. Invariably, he would arrive at and depart from the ferry landing on foot, a worn backpack patched with duct tape over his shoulder. He'd walk Chappaquiddick Road—the one paved road, the only paved road on the island—in a slow loping gait, oblivious of the joggers and cyclists, unhurried as if lost in thought.

Despite his unvarying route, no one could say for certain exactly where the man lived. Not the ferry captains. Not the FedEx driver or Angie, who delivers the mail in a cherry red Jeep. Not the young woman who runs the tiny Chappy store, the island's sole retail business, open only in July and August. Not even Gerry Jeffers, rumored to be the last surviving Wampanoag Indian on Chappaquiddick.

This uncertainty as to the Hermit's domicile was remarkable on two accounts: first because Chappaquiddick is such a small community—fewer than seventy families live here year-round. And second, because everyone on Chappaquiddick obsesses about real estate—whether or not he or she would admit it. Chappaquiddickers are keenly aware of who owns each parcel of land and deeply paranoid that the wrong person will buy the acreage adjacent to theirs. After all, you don't move to an island with three-acre zoning—without a single hotel or restaurant—

unless you want to maintain a healthy distance from your neighbors.

So who first called him the Hermit of Chappaquiddick? Perhaps it was Patrick, a twenty-year veteran of the Chappy ferry. Patrick was the quietest of the captains who piloted the *On Time II* and *On Time III*—a pair of green and white barges scarcely big enough to carry three cars and assorted bicycles and foot passengers across the 527-foot channel of water that separates Chappaquiddick Island from Edgartown and the rest of Martha's Vineyard. Patrick's mild demeanor hid a wicked sense of humor. He had a nickname for everyone who took the ferry on a more or less regular basis, and no one escaped his wit.

If there was a question as to who coined the Hermit's nickname, there was no doubt as to why. He never attended Chappy Island Association meetings or ice cream socials at the Community Center. He never appeared at Cleanup Day at the Mytoi Japanese Garden or participated in the Derby—the fishing competition that paralyzes Martha's Vineyard in the waning days of September. He never showed up at the celebrity-studded Possible Dreams Auction or at the July Fourth parade down Edgartown's Main Street. The fact is, in the ten or fifteen years the Hermit had lived on the island, he had never been seen in the company of another human being.

Naturally, no one knew what the man did for a living. You might see him with a wire clam basket in Caleb's Pond from time to time, or with a fishing rod at the Gut. Or wading in the shallow waters of Drunkard's Cove—site of a Martha's Vineyard bootleg operation during Prohibition—to gather periwinkles and scungilli. He owned a skiff, which he sometimes rowed on Cape Poge Bay. Early mornings in July, you might see him picking blueberries in the meadow at Wasque Point. But he didn't seem to be a commercial fisherman, and no one had ever seen him bring produce—either foraged or cultivated—to the local farmers' market.

When the Hermit felt sociable—that is, when he was willing to run the risk of encountering other people—he gigged for squid off the ferry dock late at night or caught crabs with a hoop net baited with fish scraps. Most often, he kept to himself. He'd build simple weirs in Chappaquiddick's salt marshes to catch eels that slithered liked sea snakes. He had set up a series of sluices and pans in a neglected corner of Poucha Pond, where he evaporated seawater into salt crystals. No one on the island had any inkling of the latter activity, for despite his ungainly appearance, the Hermit possessed a singular ability to blend into the landscape.

On the rare times when spoken to—"Nice weather" or "How's it going?"—he responded in such a low voice and in such vague terms, you had the impression you were talking to yourself. Not that anyone was aware of these evasions, for the Hermit did them in such an unassuming manner, no one paid them any heed.

The truth is that the Hermit managed to achieve the ultimate goal of any recluse. Thanks to his perpetually hunched shoulders and perennially downcast gaze, even his fellow Chappaquiddickers had long since ceased noticing him.

If you're quiet and self-effacing enough, you become invisible—perhaps even to yourself.

2

definitely served straight up

H ere's to a bad hair day," said Claire.

"Ouch," said Sheila, forcing a laugh.

They clinked glasses and Claire sloshed some chardonnay on the afghan covering her legs.

The women sprawled on a Stickley couch in front of a crackling fire in a raised fireplace in the Feinblat cottage. A cold front had swept through eastern Massachusetts, and although it was mid-July, the thermometer outside the bay window showed fifty-two degrees.

Elliott had taken Annabel and Nate to see a movie at the Edgartown Theater. Sheila and Claire were having a girls' night out at home.

Sheila's bad hair day began that morning, when a cold gray fog settled over the island, turning her flamboyant red curls into a henna-hued cloud of frizz.

Claire's bad hair day began after the first round of chemotherapy in April. Her scalp was as bare as an eggshell and she kept it wrapped in a kerchief.

Sheila poured herself and Claire another glass of wine.

The "cottage"—as such structures were called when built on Martha's Vineyard at the turn of the last century—was a gray-shingled, gambrel-roofed mansion perched high on a bluff on North Neck Road. Sheila wasn't bashful about her summer home's pedigree or its cost.

Claire knew, for example, that the architectural firm of Frederick Law Olmsted designed the house for a wealthy Boston podiatrist who invented the world's first deodorizing foot powder. That Sheila and Elliott had paid three million dollars for the property, plus another million for the renovation—the latter done by a dyspeptic contractor from West Tisbury, who frowned whenever Elliott asked him for an estimate or a price.

"Around here, people usually ask 'How soon?' not 'How much?'" the contractor said.

The money, Claire was well aware, came from the royalties of Elliott's most recent book, *It's Your Responsibility*—twenty-four weeks at the top of the *New York Times* bestseller list. The Manhattan psychiatrist earned vast sums writing about responsibility and facing the consequences. Naturally, his work sparked controversy in an age when failing students blame their teachers for not educating them better and when criminals sue prisons for the discomforts of their incarceration.

Of course, his frequent appearances on *Oprah* didn't hurt either, Sheila wasn't shy to observe. Claire's friend wasn't bashful about much.

Claire thought of her own husband, a now unemployed college professor. *Well, at least one of us married well*, she thought.

The women had been college roommates at Columbia University. Claire Doheney, the Irish Catholic from South Boston, and Sheila Feinblat, the Jewish princess from the Upper East Side in New York.

Their friends called them the Rebbetzin and the Nun.

Sheila had big hair, sensuous lips, a prodigious bust, and a personality that not only filled a room, but also barged into it. In Peter Paul Rubens's day, she would have been a pinup. Her wardrobe ran to man-tailored shirts over Lycra leggings, extravagant scarves, and dangly earrings. Imagine Queen Latifah as a white woman with a voice like Bette Midler's. If Sheila were a cocktail, it would be made in a blender and festooned with a maraschino cherry and a paper umbrella.

In healthier times, Claire had had fine chestnut hair that fell in a limp pageboy around her high cheekbones, slender nose, and delicate mouth. Her fashion tastes ran to knee-length pencil skirts and sweater sets in the pale gray green of her eyes. Claire possessed the calm of Jodie Foster and the self-deprecating charm of Diane Keaton. If she were a cocktail, it would be stirred, not shaken, and definitely served straight up.

Claire would accompany Sheila to Passover seders in the Schwartz apartment in Manhattan, where she was adopted with noisy enthusiasm. She'd read the four questions in English after one of Sheila's nephews or nieces recited them in Hebrew. She acquired a taste for gefilte fish, dosing the horseradish sauce with a heavy hand.

Sheila would spend Christmas with Claire and her mother and two sisters in their apartment in Southie, where she learned to enjoy coddle and colcannon. Sheila's mother would frown at the thought of her daughter being in the same house with a Christmas tree. "Your poor grandmother," the woman would say, "is turning over in her grave."

After college, the girls became interns at the same publishing house and roommates in an apartment in the East Village. Thirty years later, they still worked in publishing and were still best friends—survivors between them of divorces, illness, miscarriages, and corporate mergers and downsizings.

Claire worked for Apogee Press—recently acquired by the German media giant, Humboldt. She edited a highly successful biography series called Men of Action. Sheila ran the children's books division at Simpson & Smythe and had written several of the company's bestselling kids books herself.

"Well, I hope after the James Tait Black Prize they gave you a raise and corner office," Sheila said. She was referring to Britain's oldest literary award—this year bestowed on *Radiant*, a book Claire edited on the life and work of Marie Curie.

Claire shrugged at the mention of the prize and the notion of a promotion. "I'm lucky they give me a key to the bathroom," she said. "And with my treatments, I need it." Her voice grew serious. "Actually, since the merger, Beidermann has been trying to push me into early retirement. It seems the bean counters in Berlin don't like granting sick leave to patients with uncertain prognoses."

Sheila shook her head and lamented how the industry was being ruined by MBAs like Beidermann.

"You, at least, should be secure after the Disney deal with *Miss Millipede*," said Claire. The latter was a children's book Sheila had written about her daughter Annabel's bug doll—recently optioned for an animated movie.

"Honey, no one is secure in publishing these days," Sheila said. She drained the straw-colored liquid from her glass. "So what's the latest with Harrison?" She forced her voice to sound casual. It was a little game they played. Claire pretended not to want to discuss her impending divorce, and Sheila pretended to be discreet about inquiring.

"Well, it's about time!" Claire laughed. "You've only been dying to ask me since we left Manhattan."

"Well, you know us Chosen People: we don't like to be nosy," said Sheila.

"You were born nosy and you'll die nosy—and all the rhinoplasty done on Park Avenue won't change that," said Claire.

Sheila harrumphed.

"If you must know, Harrison's being a perfect prick," Claire said. "He actually threatened to sue me for alimony."

"That bastard," said Sheila.

"It gets better," said Claire. "The regents at Barnard have put him on administrative leave without pay pending a sexual harassment investigation. Turns out my beloved husband has been bedding a twenty-year-old student with boobs out to here." Claire thrust her arms out from her chest. "Her name is Jennifer—*Jennifer*, for Chrissake—and she comes from Hay Springs, Nebraska."

Claire didn't mention that the girl spoke with an odd clicking lisp—the result, she had learned, of a tongue stud.

"The buxom Jennifer has an equally buxom underage sister," Claire continued. "Apparently, Harrison left voice mail messages suggesting that a little late-night remedial reading as a threesome might help improve a less-than-stellar grade. Other girls have come forward. The Faculty Ethics Committee is having a field day." She was quiet for a minute. "How could I not have seen it?"

Love is blind, Sheila thought, but she didn't say it out loud.

"Anyway, Casanova has no income, so he figures he'll go after mine."

Claire got up and walked outside to the wraparound deck, with its unobstructed 180-degree views of Edgartown, the outer harbor, and Vineyard Sound. Off in the distance she could see glimmering lights from Cape Cod. *No wonder this place cost four million dollars.* Claire shivered in the night air, but the vista brought her rare inner calm.

Sheila joined her friend on the deck and refilled their wineglasses. "So how's Molly taking all this?" she asked.

"Oh God, Molly," Claire said. "Where do I begin?" She

took a larger sip of chardonnay than she'd meant to. "My dear daughter has shaved the hair off the sides of her head. Dyed her Mohawk cobalt blue and driven a safety pin through her septum. You should see the guys she goes out with: each one grungier than the last. And to top it off, the assistant dean called last week to ask me if there are any problems at home—apparently she's flunking out of NYU."

"Ah, the joys of motherhood," Sheila said. Earlier that day, Nate had taken a Magic Marker to Miss Millepede. His sister had a meltdown.

"So what's Molly say about Harrison?" Sheila asked.

"He can do no wrong in her eyes," Claire said. "She blames *me* for the impeding divorce. Says if I didn't have my nose in manuscripts all the time, Dad wouldn't have wandered."

"And what's Harrison say?"

"Harrison, stellar father that he is, thinks it's a good thing for a young girl to have a lot of sexual experiences. You should hear the two of them talk. It sounds like a regular Kinsey Report."

"Ouch," Sheila said.

"Ready for the best part?" Claire said. "Harrison has announced that he wants to move back into the apartment. Seems his funds are running short at the moment. Or maybe the winsome Jennifer has second thoughts about sharing a bed with the subject of a sexual harassment investigation. My lawyer says that I can't prevent him from returning without obtaining a restraining order. Both our names are on the deed—hell, legally, I can't even change the locks."

"Shit," said Sheila.

"Yeah, shit," said Claire. "Going back to all that is the last thing I need."

Sheila forced herself to sit upright. "Hey, why don't you stay here? Once school starts for the twins, I'm stuck in New York, and Elliott is supposed to spend October on a book tour in Australia."

"That's very kind, Sheila, but I couldn't," said Claire. "You and Elliott have already been so generous—"

"No, it's perfect," said Sheila. "With a phone and a DSL line, you can work anywhere. Molly and I will come visit."

"Hmm," said Claire.

"Okay, just me," said Sheila.

"What about my treatments?"

"Well, New York isn't such a far drive, or if you prefer, Elliott has an oncologist friend at the Beth Israel Hospital in Boston. You could hire a car service from Woods Hole and I'd fly up to meet you."

"I barely have a job now with all the time I've missed. Beidermann has threatened to fire me if I don't finish the Reich book by January."

"To hell with Beidermann," said Sheila. "Imagine how much work you'd get done in a quiet place like Chappaquiddick."

"What would Elliott say?"

"I'm sure he'd be thrilled to have someone we know watching the house."

"Chappaquiddick off-season? That sounds about the right speed for my love life." She thought about it some more. "Well, there's one bright spot."

Sheila looked at her quizzically.

"At least I don't have to worry about finding a hairstylist," Claire said.

When Elliott and the kids returned home, they found two empty bottles of Elliott's prized 2001 Chassagne-Montrachet and two grown women passed out on the couch.

The next morning, nursing coffees and hangovers, Sheila informed Elliott about their fall houseguest.

As she'd suspected, he rather liked the idea of having

someone besides the caretaker to look after the cottage. He called his friend at Beth Israel. Yes, they could continue the treatment protocol in Boston. As it turned out, the oncologist had trained with Claire's doctor in Manhattan. Sheila found a car service that would take Claire to Boston and back every three weeks.

As far as Elliott was concerned, there was just one final detail to attend to. When the women went shopping in Edgartown later that week, Elliott moved the remaining bottles of Chassagne-Montrachet to a locked cupboard in the basement. He put some less pedigreed chardonnay where the women would find it for their next girls' night.

Elliott was a giving man, but there were limits to even his generosity.

3

plenty of time

It was his favorite time of day—the hour before dawn. He loved the way the darkness dissolved into indigo, then mauve, then lavender, then finally the brilliant gold of sunrise. He loved how the silence of night gave way to the rippling waves and splashing sea life, the wind soughing through the pine trees.

But most of all, the Hermit loved this time of day because he knew he would be alone.

Few of the island's summer residents awoke early enough to see the sunrise. The hordes of tourists from Edgartown wouldn't descend on Chappaquiddick until the sun was high in the sky.

The Hermit stood on a wooden bridge spanning the narrow channel that led from Poucha Pond to Cape Poge Bay. The outgoing tide made rippling sounds against the pilings. A pair of egrets rose from the marsh grass in a noisy flapping of wings. Off in the distance, the surf boomed against East Beach and if you had good eyesight, you might still see a glimmering light or two on Nantucket, fifteen miles to the east.

The Hermit breathed in the sea air deeply and exhaled with visible pleasure. The breeze billowed his shirttails and tousled his silvery hair.

The Dyke Bridge is the most famous landmark on Chappaquiddick. Even if you've never been to Martha's Vineyard, you're probably aware of what happened here on the evening of July 18, 1969. Overhead in the dark sky, a spacecraft called Apollo 11 sped toward the moon. Down on the island, a black Oldsmobile roared up an unlit dirt road toward the beach. The driver lost control as he crossed the bridge and careened into the water.

The accident had two immediate consequences: The United States Senator driving the car lost any real chance of achieving his lifelong presidential aspirations. And a smart, personable, blond, blue-eyed, twenty-eight-year-old woman lost her life.

The Hermit made his way to a plastic barrel he had buried in the marsh grass. Had you been nearby, you would have recoiled at the reek of rotten fish as the Hermit pried off the lid. The odor was no accident—it was the result of a careful fermentation of herring heads and Pocha Pond sea salt. The Hermit had layered these ingredients in proportions he had painstakingly worked out over the years and left the fish to ferment for several weeks in the hot sun.

The result was an effluvium that smelled slightly better than a week-old corpse and slightly worse than just about anything else. But for one of God's creatures—*Homarus americanus*, the American lobster—it was the sweetest scent in the world. Had the Hermit been alive when the Pilgrims arrived in Massachusetts, he wouldn't have needed such malodorous bait.

Back then, lobsters were so plentiful, he knew, you could fill a bushel bucket simply by wading into the water.

Had you asked the Hermit the origin of the word *lobster*, he would have cited the Latin *locusta*, literally "locust." The Hermit loved etymologies and word histories. The connection survives today in a locution used by lobstermen throughout New England. They call their catch *bugs*.

On the morning of July 19, 1969, two Chappaquiddick boys awoke at dawn to go fishing off the Dyke Bridge. Their hooks snagged neither bugs nor bluefish, but a black Oldsmobile under twelve feet of water. The previous evening, the senator had been partying at a cottage on Chappaquiddick Road. The night was dark and moonless, he testified later; he must have taken a wrong turn. He dived in the water repeatedly, but his passenger seemed to have vanished.

Most of the tourists who flock to the site of the tragedy are surprised by its modest dimensions. The Dyke Bridge is so short, you can walk across it in twenty seconds, and so narrow, cars driving on or off the beach must wait their turn to pass single file. (Contrary to a popular misconception, the bridge does *not* connect Chappaquiddick to the rest of Martha's Vineyard—it's a shortcut to a strip of barrier beach on the eastern edge of the island.) Today, there are thick wooden posts and cable guardrails, and it's hard to imagine driving recklessly enough to crash through them. There were no guard wires, the Hermit knew, in 1969.

The Hermit kept a half dozen lobster traps in the outer reaches of Cape Poge Bay, and once a week, he checked them. He walked to a weathered skiff hidden in the eelgrass beyond the bridge pilings. If ever the boat had had a name, the letters had long since worn off. So had the Coast Guard registration numbers. Once the boat had had an outboard motor—a ninety-horsepower Evinrude. The intake valve sucked up a plastic bag one day and the engine overheated and seized. The Hermit never bothered to repair it. He had plenty of time—what difference did it make if he motored or rowed to the lobster traps?

The senator, it seemed, had had plenty of time, too. After the accident, he walked the three miles back to the Chappy ferry landing, swam across Edgartown Harbor, and made a highly visible appearance in his hotel lobby at 2:30 A.M. He also made sixteen phone calls—none of them to the local authorities. In fact, the senator had so much time, it took him ten hours to report the accident to the police.

Chappaquiddick supplied the Hermit with far more than his dietary needs. He cut white oak for his heating and cooking and lit his firewood with local pitch pine. He illuminated his home with candles made from sweet-scented bayberries, which grow in profusion throughout Martha's Vineyard. If he cut himself, he packed the wound with sphagnum moss. To ward off colds and scurvy, he chewed uncooked local cranberries. When the Hermit had a cough or headache, he made tea from the bark of wild cherry.

The Hermit was a practical man: if he didn't take care of himself, who would?

The senator's headache required a remedy stronger than medicinal tea. A war council was convened at the family compound in nearby Hyannis Port. The senator wound up pleading guilty to leaving the scene of an accident and operating a motor vehicle in a reckless manner. He received a two-month sentence at the House of Correction in Barnstable on Cape Cod. The jail time was later suspended.

And gradually, the tragedy was put to rest, as was the memory of a woman who died two years shy of her thirtieth birthday.

The Hermit, too, it turns out, had flouted the laws of the Commonwealth of Massachusetts. All these years he set lobster traps, and he had never bothered to apply for a license.

4

big in courage

S hit," said Claire as she watched the ferry pull away from the dock at the Steamship Authority Terminal in Woods Hole.

It had been a bad day.

Claire had spent the morning at the Beth Israel Deaconess Medical Center in Boston receiving near toxic doses of a drug designed to crash the genetic programs that govern the growth rate of cancer cells. The port below her shoulder had stopped working, as they sometimes do after a few months, so they had to start a drip in her arm. Claire's regular nurse was home with the flu. A student nurse attempted to insert the needle; it took her four tries to hit the vein. "I feel like a pincushion," Claire said with a wan smile. She tried to put the poor girl at ease.

The book editor sat in a Barcalounger in the chemotherapy center surrounded by the usual sea of sad faces. A manuscript lay unread on her lap. The room echoed with the sounds of strained conversations, fussing babies, and the chatter of a dozen mini TV sets. Claire held an orange to her nose—a trick she had learned from one of the nurses to mask the smell of the disinfectants. She stared at a blank TV screen in front of her while the medication dripped into her arm. Sheila had left a message with the head nurse: She had planned to fly to Boston to join Claire, but a thunderstorm grounded her plane at LaGuardia.

The town car was late. The driver claimed he went to the wrong entrance at the hospital to meet her. The rain from New York had arrived in Boston, and the cars on Route 3 sat bumper to bumper. They pulled up at the Steamship Authority terminal in Woods Hole just as the white stern of the *Island Home*—the last boat of the evening to Martha's Vineyard—disappeared into the darkness.

Claire went to use the restroom in the terminal. The driver, who was late for another job, dumped her suitcase by the entrance and departed. A thunderclap sounded and a lightning bolt split the sky. Claire dragged her bag to three inns in downtown Woods Hole, but all had NO VACANCY signs in the windows.

Rain started to fall—first a drizzle, then a downpour. In a matter of minutes, she was drenched.

"It's the Upper Cape 30K Bike Race this weekend," the third innkeeper explained. "You won't find a room anywhere between Woods Hole and Hyannis."

"Shit," said Claire.

It had been a bad week.

As he had threatened, Harrison demanded to be let back into the apartment. He backed up his claim with a court-issued order from a Family Court judge. The judge was a middle-aged woman with frosted hair and a Botoxed forehead. Harrison flirted so shamelessly with her, even his lawyer was embarrassed. Harrison explained that since he was on unpaid leave from the college, he couldn't afford to rent another apartment. His wife was living in

Massachusetts, he said, so there was no reason he shouldn't be allowed to return to what, legally after all, was still his home.

Sheila rushed to the apartment to clear out Claire's personal papers. She caught Harrison in *flagrante delicto* in the couple's bed with a woman young enough to be his daughter.

"Shit," said Claire.

It had been a bad month.

Molly had come for a visit. A half dozen new piercings—spikes, hoops, wires—protruded from her ears and nostrils. The boyfriend in tow this month was a nervous nineteen-year-old named Snort. The first thing Snort did on arriving was to help himself to two bottles of Elliott's prized Ommegang Hennepin Belgian-style ale.

Claire quickly learned how the boy—whose real name was Stuart—got his nickname. Every few hours, Snort would disappear into the bathroom. He'd return a few minutes later—pupils dilated—and would launch into a jittery monologue about all the great things he would accomplish if only he got a break. Snort had the ability to talk for hours on end without once coming to the point. He finally passed out after being awake for thirty-six hours, but not before propping his boots on the afghan.

"You know you're always welcome wherever I am," Claire told Molly. "But you can't continue to bring these lowlifes into our friends' home."

"You don't love me," Molly whined.

For once, Claire found it hard to persuade her daughter otherwise.

It had been a bad year.

She and Harrison had decided to stay home last New Year's Eve. They ate Chinese carryout from cartons in front of the television and made love just as the illuminated Waterford crystal ball descended the façade of the Times Square Building. Claire didn't know it that night, but it was the last time she would ever have sex with her husband.

The next morning, as Claire was taking a shower, she thought she felt a small lump in her armpit. She called for Harrison to feel it.

"I'm on the phone," he called out from the bedroom.

They went to New Year's Day brunch with the Feinblats. Claire hardly touched her food. Later, when Claire lay in bed, try as she could, she could not find the lump again.

"Probably just my imagination," she murmured to Harrison, who had fallen asleep reading.

But when she took a shower the following day, it was there, and now she thought she felt a lump in her left breast. She called her gynecologist.

The doctor palpated Claire's breasts and armpits. "There's something here, but it might just be a cyst or fibroid," he said. "Sometimes it's hard to detect lumps in women who are firm and petite." He tried to sound reassuring, but to Claire, he didn't seem convinced. Maybe he didn't want to be the one to break the bad news. The doctor scribbled a name on a prescription pad. "You need to see this woman. She's where I'd send my wife if she needed a specialist."

But Claire couldn't get an appointment for another two weeks. By the time she took the elevator in the Sloan-Kettering medical office building, she was frantic with worry. She hadn't told anyone close to her about the scare. Harrison seemed to have nonstop business on campus. (Department chair search and midterm grade crunch, he said.) Sheila and Elliott were off in Venice. And Molly was acting out enough already without adding the stress of a sick parent.

As Claire walked down the hallway, with its scuffed floors and medicinal smells, the despair from legions of the lame and infirm was almost palpable. "Maybe it's nothing," she told herself—as she had a thousand times in the last weeks. As if wishful thinking could effect a cure.

NEFERTITI GUPTA, ONCOLOGIST read the sign next to the door to the office. All that was missing, Claire thought, was an inscription on the lintel from Dante:

ABANDON ALL HOPE, YE WHO ENTER HERE.

Dr. Gupta had kindly eyes, curly gray hair, paisley eyeglasses on a gold chain, and skin the color of milk chocolate. Her smile lit her face like a halogen lamp. There was something about her calm manner that put Claire instantly at ease. Dr. Gupta had been born in Cairo of Indian parents, raised in Calcutta, and educated at Oxford, she said by way of explaining her curious name and accent. She spoke with the wide vowels and rolling consonants of the Indian subcontinent, and when she said the word *oncology*, she managed to make it sound like a position in the *Kama Sutra*.

Dr. Gupta had one other remarkable attribute: she stood only three feet ten inches tall. Dr. Gupta was a dwarf.

The doctor looked at Claire's X-rays and frowned. She stood on a wooden box, palpated Claire's breasts and upper body, and frowned some more.

"I feel something here," she said, guiding Claire's hand instantly to the very spot with the pea-shaped lump in her armpit that had proved so elusive. "And here," she touched Claire's left breast. "And possibly here," she said, touching Claire's right breast.

Dr. Gupta took Claire's hand. "You were wise to come see me, Claire," she said. "We need to do a biopsy."

Most people alive at the time remember exactly where they were and what they were doing the moment they learned that President Kennedy had been assassinated. And most people vividly remember similar details surrounding the instant American Airlines Flight 11 slammed into the North Tower of the World Trade Center.

Time becomes frozen the same way, with all the immutable details, when a woman learns she has breast cancer.

Claire returned to see Dr. Gupta two days later. As she sat in the doctor's office, she was acutely aware of the time (3:04 P.M.), the logo on the coffee cup on the doctor's desk (Dean & Deluca), the headline of *The New York Times* that morning (CAR BOMB KILLS 60 IN KARBALA), and the weather (a gray sky with a light drizzle). She certainly remembered the date, for it was February 14, Valentine's Day.

Dr. Gupta came around the desk, stood on her box, and put a hand on Claire's shoulder. "Claire, I'm afraid I have some bad news for you. The biopsies we took are positive. You have breast cancer. I'm sorry. But awful as that seems, it's an illness, not a death sentence."

"Will I lose my breasts?" Claire asked.

"I don't know yet," Dr. Gupta said. "I will do everything in my power so you don't." Then, seeing tears well up in Claire's eyes, the diminutive doctor made the following observation: "God makes some people big in height and some people big in wisdom. Claire Doheney, I sense that God has made you big in courage."

When Claire returned home, she was one shade paler than snow—except for her eyes, which were the red of a Valentine's Day rose from weeping. She found Harrison dressed in a tie and jacket and reeking of Armani cologne.

"I thought we agreed we'd stay home this evening," said Claire. "Harrison, I have something to tell you: I have breast cancer."

Harrison came round to face her, but didn't touch her. "This is really bad timing, but I have something to tell you, too, Claire: I'm in love with another woman."

He picked up his coat and walked out the door, and her husband of twenty-one years was gone.

5

a "disinhabited iland"

The Hermit stood at Cape Poge Point and watched the waves crash into the shoreline. The clouds lay low and leaden, like a gray blanket hung from the sky.

Four hundred years earlier, another man watched the waves crash into the same shore. From his vantage point, however, the horizon seemed to rock wildly up and down. He stood on the deck of a wooden ship called the *Concord*. His name was Bartholomew Gosnold, and he had sailed from England to make his fortune in the New World.

The Hermit had come to this secluded stretch of beach on an intuition. As he gazed up shore, he could see his hunch hit the mark. A couple hundred yards up the beach, a swarm of seagulls wheeled noisily over a large dark mass at the edge of the water.

Captain Gosnold had come here on a hunch, too—but his

missed by a hundred miles. He was looking for a "happy beautiful bay with many islands and friendly Indians," described by an earlier explorer, Giovanni da Verrazzano. Instead of sailing to Narragansett Bay in what would later become Rhode Island, however, he landed on Chappaquiddick.

Unaware of his error, Gosnold dispatched a small landing party to explore this new land. The men found woods, vines, gooseberries, raspberries, and all manner of wild fowl and game, but no signs of human life. "A place most fair" is how the ship's journal keeper, Gabriel Archer, described Chappaquiddick. And having encountered no "savages," as the English called the locals at the time, Archer pronounced it "a disinhabited Iland." The date was May 22, 1602.

The Hermit often found interesting things on the upper reaches of Cape Poge. A ship's bell from an old schooner shipwrecked off East Beach in the 1890s. Whiskey bottles ditched by a Martha's Vineyard rumrunner during a Coast Guard raid in the Prohibition years. The seawater had long since washed off the labels and corroded the metal caps, but the whiskey made for excellent sipping. Once he even found live ordnance—an unexploded practice bomb dropped on Cape Poge by a navy pilot on a training run from Onset, Rhode Island, during World War II. The Hermit spent a week figuring out how to disarm it so it wouldn't explode and cause harm.

There was very little the Hermit couldn't figure out when he put his mind to it.

The Hermit walked along the beach toward the dark mass and the whirling gulls. He sniffed as he approached. A cool wind blew in the pungent scent of a large sea mammal. The form of the mass grew distinct: it was a pilot whale. It was hardly the leviathan depicted in *Moby-Dick* or even the size of the black metal whale tail sculpture in the park next to the Old Sculpin Gallery in Edgartown.

Even so, the Hermit reckoned it stretched twelve feet from

the tip of its blunt head to its crescent-shaped tail and weighed one and one-half tons. Apparently, the whale had swum deliberately with, not against, the incoming tide and had beached itself on Chappaquiddick. For reasons unknown to the Hermit or to the legions of marine biologists who study such behavior, it had tried to commit suicide.

In pronouncing Chappaquiddick "disinhabited," Gosnold and company made another blunder. The island was anything but. Hidden behind tall oak trees and watching these strange pale-skinned creatures was a band of Wampanoag Indians. They called their island Noepe ("place in the midst of the water," literally), and their tribe had lived here for more than a millennium.

Later that week, Gosnold and crew met face-to-face with some Wampanoags at Lambert's Cove, ten miles or so up island. They displayed that odd mixture of self-righteousness and condescending bonhomie typical of so many encounters between the Europeans and the natives. The Indians had never seen facial hair like that worn by the Englishmen; they offered to buy their beards. The Englishmen gave the Wampanoags a taste of English mustard. The Indians' howls of discomfort made the sailors slap their knees with delight.

The laughter stopped a few days later, when a party of Gosnold's men came across a Wampanoag canoe on a neighboring islet. They did what most Europeans had felt free to do with just about anything they found in the New World: They stole it. The Wampanoags reacted with understandable anger to the theft of a vessel that had taken several men several weeks to carve from a single log using techniques little changed since the Stone Age. The erstwhile friends of the Englishmen let fly a volley of arrows, one of which wounded a *Concord* crew member. No laughing matter, indeed.

The Wampanoags had many physical advantages over their English visitors: They were bigger, taller, healthier, and had better, whiter teeth. They lived longer than the average Englishman of the day and were free of such diseases as syphilis and smallpox. They smelled better than the English, who, on average, took a bath only once a year.

They also lived in remarkable harmony with their island—catching fish, digging bivalves, hunting game, gathering a cornucopia of edible and medicinal wild plants—many of the same consumed by the Hermit. But idyllic as this existence was, the Wampanoags had one fatal flaw: Their culture lacked the concept of private property.

The Hermit waved his hands to shoo away the gulls. He bent down to examine the pilot whale. Its eyes looked glassy and bright; its body rose and fell almost imperceptibly in a movement that suggested respiration. It was still alive. Had the Hermit been a Wampanoag, he would have done what any reasonable man did when the Great Spirit sent a large unexpected parcel of food your way. He would have clubbed the animal to death, cut the blubber into strips, gorged on some raw on the spot, and sizzled the remainder in a pot to render the whale oil.

The Wampanoags weren't the only islanders to recognize the benefits of whales. Like most coastal towns in New England, Edgartown once sent out fleets of whaling ships—sixteen in the year of 1841 alone. At the height of the whaling era, a full half of Martha's Vineyard's young men between the ages of fourteen and nineteen took to the sea. Whaling voyages lasted three to four years, and the wealth from their cargo built the stately sea captains' mansions in Edgartown. At least one Martha's Vineyard whaler, a Gay Head Indian named Tashtego, was immortalized in *Moby-Dick*.

The Hermit always traveled with an Opinel pocketknife and a walking stick. This morning he also carried a burlap bag for foraging and a bucket. He stepped back from the whale and looked at it for a while. What he did next would surely have seemed incomprehensible to a Wampanoag.

He cut open the burlap bag and draped it over the pilot whale's head. Then he walked to the surf several times to fill the bucket with seawater, which he poured over the burlap to soak it. He patted the whale on its head, then walked in his slow loping gait to the Trustees of Reservations office at Mytoi Garden. He scribbled a note describing the whale's predicament and exact location and left it where a ranger was sure to find it.

If you picked up a copy of the *Vineyard Gazette* the following week, you would have read about the heroic efforts of a group of Martha's Vineyard High School seniors to keep a pilot whale beached on Chappaquiddick cool and hydrated until it could be floated out to sea on the next high tide. The effort lasted three days, but in the end, when a whale wants to die, it will die, and all the goodwill on the part of another species of mammal can't save it.

The article did not mention the anonymous note that initiated the rescue effort. It did report with no small reprobation that, after the dead whale's body washed up back on Chappaquiddick a few days later, the carcass had been flayed with a knife. And that next to it lay the remains of a campfire. "Desecrating a dead animal's carcass this way is barbaric," read one letter to the editor. "Utterly unworthy of the conservational spirit of the Vineyard," read another. The Hermit knew nothing of this, of course, for he didn't read the newspapers.

As for Captain Gosnold, he had no desire to deal with hostile Indians. Despite his intentions to establish a trading post here, he decided to return to England. The trip wasn't a complete bust, for the good captain had managed to load the hold of the *Concord* with a plant that grew—and still grows—in great profusion on Chappaquiddick. Its mitten-shaped leaves and root beer–scented bark and roots were in great demand, thanks to a disease ravaging Europe at the time. The plant was sassafras, and Gosnold's contemporaries believed it could cure the French pox, better known today as syphilis.

Before weighing anchor to return home, Captain Gosnold did one other thing that would have lasting significance for the island. Mindful of the wild grapes his men found growing in abundance—and of the infant daughter he had left back in England and whom he hoped to hold in his arms again soon—he named the place Martha's Vineyard.

6

her new life

C laire settled into what she had come to regard as her new life. She woke at daybreak and went to bed at 10 P.M. When the weather permitted (and it did most of that radiant fall), she took her coffee on the deck overlooking Vineyard Sound. In the mornings, she edited manuscripts. Afternoons, she took long walks around Chappaquiddick and Edgartown.

She bought side baskets for her bicycle and crossed the bike on the ferry. She'd ride along Main Street, past the Daniel Fisher House with its white Federal-style portico and shiny black shutters, past the Old Whaling Church with its massive wooden columns and square four-spire steeple. She grocery shopped at Stop & Shop and enrolled in a yoga class at the gym at the Edgartown Triangle. She attended weekly Breast Cancer

Survivor Meetings at the Martha's Vineyard Hospital in Vineyard Haven.

Claire would go days at a time without crossing the harbor to Edgartown—yet she never felt bored. She often went forty-eight hours without seeing another human being—yet she never felt lonely. When she did run into a fellow islander during one of her long walks, a simple hello and the exchange of a few pleasantries about the weather seemed as satisfying as an intense Manhattan conversation.

After Harrison moved out, Claire had felt self-conscious about going to a restaurant or movie alone in New York. Here, she was perfectly comfortable seeing a film at the Edgartown Theater by herself or dining solo at the bar at Alchemy. One evening, a man seated next to her struck up a conversation and offered to buy her a drink.

Claire enjoyed spending time in Edgartown, but was always eager to return to the tranquility of Chappaquiddick. One night, as she drove home during a thunderstorm, she passed a man walking alone along Chappaquiddick Road. His shoulders were hunched in a waterlogged coat and rainwater dripped from his hair. She pulled the car to the side of the road and asked if he wanted a ride. He looked at her blankly, then shook his head and walked on.

Claire set up an office in the Feinblat cottage in a spare bedroom overlooking the harbor. The FedEx truck would pull into the shell-lined driveway several times a week to bring her galleys or page proofs from the Apogee offices in TriBeCa.

She spoke to Beidermann by phone as seldom as possible—an arrangement that suited both of them. If Claire stayed on Martha's Vineyard, Beidermann reasoned, perhaps he could change her status to that of consultant. That would free the company from the considerable expense of her health insurance and paid sick leave. But even the calculating Beidermann couldn't quite bring himself to discontinue Claire's coverage while his star editor was fighting cancer.

One morning, a high-pitched car horn shattered the air. Claire emerged from the house to watch a preposterously tall slender man with bushy white hair and bottlebrush eyebrows and mustache extricate himself from the confines of a Volkswagen Beetle. He wore a rumpled linen suit with a bow tie, thick wool socks, and Birkenstocks. It was one of her authors, Ely Samuelson, freshly arrived from Maine.

Claire rushed to give him a welcoming hug and help him with his luggage. The latter consisted of a small backpack with his clothing and toiletries, an Igloo cooler, and four large cardboard file boxes filled with papers. Claire prayed the latter were not all manuscript.

When most people arrive at the Feinblat estate, they rush to the edge of the cliff and stand slack-jawed, admiring the view of Edgartown Harbor. Ely seemed oblivious of the waterfront setting. He looked deeply into Claire's eyes for what felt to her like several minutes. For Ely, human connections were more important than the surroundings. His gaze seemed to search her soul.

"You've gained weight," he said with a nod of approval. "It becomes you."

"So that's why you're still a bachelor!" Claire laughed. She scolded Ely that most women would *not* regard noticing a weight gain as a compliment.

But Claire had gained weight and it was one of the more surprising side effects of chemotherapy. The treatments left Claire feeling as though there was an empty pit in her stomach. She ate constantly in an effort to fill it. She would cook bountiful meals for herself for three or four days after treatment. Then a few days of wretched nausea would set in and Claire couldn't bear even to look at food. Once the nausea abated, she found herself trying to fill the pit again.

Ely Samuelson had come to Claire's office in New York a year earlier to propose a biography of the iconoclastic psychiatrist, Wilhelm Reich. Claire racked her brain to recall something favorable about Reich, but all that came to mind were vague recollections of a kooky psychotherapist who ran afoul of the law by making his patients sit in some sort of controversial box.

She cleared a stack of galleys from the chair in front of her desk and motioned for Ely to sit. Ely looked nervously at the papers and books piled precariously on Claire's desk and bookshelves.

Claire asked Ely two questions she asked all her potential authors: Why should she or any reader care about the subject's life? And what made Ely uniquely qualified to write about it?"

Ely spoke about Reich's evolution—from traditional Freudian psychoanalyst to Marxist revolutionary, sexologist, biologist, and natural scientist. "Dr. Reich's research led him to fields of inquiry that most experts relegated to the realm of science fiction," explained Ely. His eyebrows rose to express a fascination undimmed in the half century since Reich's death.

"Have you ever heard of primal scream therapy, encounter groups, bioenergetics, and psychodrama?" Ely asked Claire, bouncing in his seat with excitement. "All have their roots in Reich's work." The bottlebrush mustache arched with the enthusiasm of a squad of cheerleaders at a football game.

"And your interest in Reich?" asked Claire.

By now, Ely was on his feet, pacing among the stacks of books on the floor.

"When I was eighteen, I started therapy with Dr. Reich," said Ely. "Eventually, I became one of his assistants, and I spent two years at his research center in Rangeley, Maine." Here the eyebrows and mustache did a ballet that reminded Claire of the pas de deux preceding Odette's death in *Swan Lake*.

Claire looked at her watch and realized she and Ely had

been talking for two hours. She was supposed to meet with Beidermann at noon. She asked her assistant to call to say she was running late.

"Any other qualifications besides your personal involvement with Dr. Reich?" asked Claire.

It turned out that Ely had a Ph.D. in psychology from Harvard and was a board-certified psychotherapist specializing in Reichian and bioenergetic techniques. He edited two scientific journals with admittedly minuscule circulations, and a few years back had written a vegan cookbook.

"You know, Ely, these sorts of books rarely make much money for either the writer or the publishing house," said Claire. She folded her hands on her desk.

"Consider it a labor of love," said Ely, and his eyebrows lowered as though they were taking a bow.

Then Claire did something that reminded her of the old days of publishing, back before the arrival of MBAs like Beidermann, when editors ran their imprints like personal fiefdoms. She offered Ely a ten-thousand-dollar advance for the Reich biography—without submitting the newly required acquisition memo.

"Beidermann will have apoplexy," she told Sheila after Ely left—especially for a book on a renegade like Reich.

"Claire Doheney has made Apogee a lot of money over the years," Sheila said. "Beidermann will get over it."

Claire walked Ely into the house and showed him to a bedroom behind the Feinblat library. She helped him carry the file boxes to her office. He opened the cooler and asked Claire to put its contents in the refrigerator. She arranged the nine jars in the Sub-Zero and gave him a puzzled look.

"Sauerkraut," said Ely.

Ely was as eccentric in his eating habits, it turned out, as Reich had been in his practice of psychotherapy. Ely was always coming up with strange new theories about what constituted the healthiest diet. Usually, this involved eating a single food for breakfast, lunch, and dinner for months on end—until a new food, deemed even more salubrious—replaced it.

When Claire took Ely out to lunch at the Union Square Cafe in New York to celebrate the book deal, he ordered curried tomato soup, an heirloom tomato salad, a fried-green-tomato napoleon as a main course, and tomato sorbet for dessert. A month later, the tomato regimen gave way to an all–Andean quinoa diet, then to citrus fruits consumed rind and all. For one six-month period, Ely ate nothing but an Indonesian wheat gluten product called tempeh.

The next morning Claire was jolted from her coffee by a series of bloodcurdling screams and thumps. The noise emanated from Ely's bedroom behind the library. It sounded like a botched homicide.

Claire rushed to the door and knocked. "Ely, are you okay?"

"Okay!" Ely shouted, panting, through the door. The thumps accelerated in tempo to a crescendo, which was accompanied by a loud drawn-out scream.

A half hour later, a freshly showered and energized Ely walked into the kitchen and took a jar of sauerkraut from the refrigerator.

"For breakfast?" Claire winced.

Ely crunched his sauerkraut as though it were the tastiest granola imaginable and spurned Claire's freshly brewed coffee. He considered all caffeinated beverages toxic.

The noises, he explained to Claire, resulted from a series of exercises devised by Alexander Lowen. A disciple of Reich, Dr. Lowen founded of a school of psychotherapy called bioenergetics.

The exercises consisted of lying on your back and pounding the mattress with your fists, then kicking like a child having a temper tantrum. They were designed to release blocked emotions and restore the energy flow in the body.

"You should try it sometime," said Ely. "I'd be happy to show you."

Claire gave silent thanks that her nearest neighbor lived a quarter mile away, safely out of earshot.

After breakfast, they moved to Claire's office, where Ely began to arrange neatly labeled file folders in piles.

"So how do you tell the story of someone's life?" Claire mused out loud, as much for herself as for Ely.

The most obvious way is to organize the narrative chronologically, Claire explained, which after all, is how people actually live their lives. This approach suits a grand artist like Leonardo da Vinci, who produced works of genius and found himself in situations of controversy almost every year of his life.

Other life stories might be better told, Claire observed, if you tackled the subject thematically. For example, you could make a case for narrating Picasso's life through his various artistic periods: cubism, surrealism, blue, abstract, and so on. The risk here, she cautioned, was that the work of the genius tended to overshadow the life of the man.

Ely pondered this for a few minutes. As he thought, he paced. As he paced, he pulled at his mustache, and his eyebrows raised and lowered.

"I think we should present Reich's life in terms of energy and motion. Reich was a restless man," Ely explained. "He lived and worked in six countries on two continents." Even in his final home—the U.S.—his research took him from New York to Maine to Arizona. More important, Ely said, it was Reich's obsession with energy—thought streams in the mind; energy streams in the body and nature—that led to what Reich considered to be his most important discovery—and his ultimate personal undoing—a cosmic force he called orgone energy.

Ely and Claire agreed that the final chapter would explore

Reich's intellectual legacy in the fields of psychology and social science.

They worked until noon, then broke for lunch, which for Ely consisted of another jar of sauerkraut. They worked some more; then Claire sent Ely on a walk to the ferry and Edgartown to pick up some groceries.

"So how's your author?" Sheila asked when Claire phoned her later that afternoon.

"Brilliant as the Harvard graduate he is," Claire said. "And nutty as a fruitcake."

She changed the subject. "Do you remember that bizarre soup your mother used to make with sauerkraut?"

"Watch it," said Sheila. "You're talking about a sacred Schwartz family recipe."

"How do you make it?" Claire asked.

An hour later, the scent of sautéed onion, garlic, celery, and carrot filled the Feinblat kitchen. Ely allowed Claire to add some beef short ribs to the soup for flavor, provided she removed the meat from his portion. In went the sauerkraut and juices, some beef stock, a bay leaf, and a whole clove stuck in a strip of lemon zest. Claire added enough brown sugar to offset the acidity of the sauerkraut. At least she hoped it would—from time to time, she suffered from dysgeusia, a side effect of chemotherapy that made sweet flavors taste sour or salty flavors taste sweet. She served the steaming soup in bowls with heaping dollops of sour cream and hoped for the best.

Ely pronounced it delectable—although perhaps not completely within the spirit of his diet. Claire asked about Reich's eating habits. The eyebrows went up as Ely searched his memory and fell when he could not produce a single notable culinary reminiscence.

"In the last difficult years of his life, he often ate out of cans," said Ely. "I guess you'd have to say he ate to live, not lived to eat." Claire's opinion of the psychiatric iconoclast dropped.

By the third morning of Ely's visit, Claire had grown accustomed to the thumps and screams. After breakfast, they finished outlining the major events of Reich's life. He was born on March 24, 1897, the son of a major landholder in Galicia. He died at the age of sixty in a federal penitentiary in Pennsylvania. Along the way, he fought with the Austrian army on the Italian front in World War I, marched with the Communist Party in Weimar Germany, moved to Norway to flee the Nazis, and corresponded with Albert Einstein.

It was a tumultuous life in a cataclysmic century lived by a man in whom, in Ely's opinion, genius and madness were locked in a heroic struggle.

Then Claire made two suggestions that confirmed to Ely that he had chosen the right editor.

"The first is the oldest trick in the biographer's book," she explained, "but it never fails to grab a reader's interest." She suggested Ely start his biography at the end of Reich's life—his imprisonment—then flash back to his childhood and work forward through his controversial career, building to the events that lead to his incarceration.

The second was for Ely to weave his own story into Reich's. "What was it like to be in therapy with Reich?" she asked. "How did he speak to you? What did his voice sound like? What did he ask you to do? Did he give you what you wanted or needed? Did he ever let you down?"

Harrison came to her mind for a moment. She pushed the thought away.

"This is something you, Ely, bring to a Reich biography that no one else can," Claire said. "Make the reader feel like he's interacting with a flesh-and-blood human being, and you will write a compelling biography—no matter who is the subject."

With that, Claire packed three jars of sauerkraut soup in the cooler for Ely's journey back to Maine and helped him stuff the folders back into the file boxes. They agreed to meet again in a month. Claire watched him fold his tall frame, origami-like, into the driver's seat of the Volkswagen, and with a high-pitched honk of the horn, he drove off.

7

like a crumpled rag doll

*L*ooks like a crumpled rag doll, the Hermit thought when he saw her. *Like a pile of laundry strewn by the side of the road.* Summer folk were always losing their possessions—a child's sweater or a stuffed animal tumbled to the ground from a bike basket. Or a bag of dirty bedclothes bounced off the back of a Jeep on its way to the Edgartown Laundromat.

One time, the Hermit found a suitcase in the middle of Litchfield Road. It must have rattled loose from a car roof rack. Most of Chappaquiddick has bumpy dirt roads. Even Chappaquiddick Road—the only paved road on the island—dwindles to dirt on the way to Wasque Point.

The Hermit moved the suitcase to the side of the road, where it remained unclaimed for three days. At that point, he felt free to scavenge its contents. In so doing, he joined a long line of "wreckers"—Martha's Vineyarders who helped themselves to the cargoes of the numerous shipwrecks that had washed up on Chappaquiddick's East Beach over the past four centuries. The suitcase yielded three unworn flannel shirts, a new pair of jeans, and pair of L.L. Bean lug boots, which he incorporated into his wardrobe.

It was five in the morning, and the Hermit was walking along North Neck Road, on his way to a small park owned by the Sheriff's Meadow Foundation. A cool mist rose from the damp earth and the moon was full—perfect fishing conditions for bluefish.

Bluefish is, perhaps, Martha's Vineyard's most misunderstood seafood—adored by the people who catch it and reviled by just about everyone else. The reason has to do with the fish's singular position on the food chain. Moving "like a pack of wolves" (in the words of a nineteenth-century fisheries expert), bluefish eat twice their weight in other fish each day; feeding schools have been known to chase their prey clear up on dry land. Their powerful digestive enzymes make bluefish taste unpleasantly "fishy" when less than impeccably fresh.

The good news, as any Martha's Vineyard fisherman knows, is that when bluefish is eaten within a few hours of being caught, there is no sweeter, moister, meatier morsel in God's oceans. It was bluefish that brought the Hermit to North Neck Road early this November morning.

The northern end of Chappaquiddick—Cape Poge—curves around and back on itself in a slender hook, like a fishhook. The end of this hook comes within forty yards of another slender strip of land called North Neck. The locals call the narrow gap between them "the Gut."

Thanks to a principle of fluid dynamics first described by the Dutch mathematician Daniel Bernoulli, water coming through the Gut flows in a hard, fast, cold, powerful current. From a bluefish's point of view, these make perfect conditions for feeding. The Hermit had made some mathematical calculations of his own, and they told him that with the full moon and high tide reaching the Gut around 6 A.M., the blues should be biting like crazy.

Such were the Hermit's thoughts—and he rather enjoyed them—when he came upon the woman lying in North Neck Road. No, it wasn't an oversized Raggedy Ann. Closer examination revealed a pink Martha's Vineyard sweatshirt, blue jeans, a fringed shawl, and a blue and gold kerchief. The shawl and slim frame suggested a female, although the headscarf had slipped off to reveal a bald head.

A bicycle lay on the ground next to her. A few inches from the woman's head was a stone. Groceries spilled from the bicycle's side baskets onto the road. A line of deer tracks jagged across the sandy dirt road a few feet away, completing the tableau. The woman must have been startled by the deer and lost control of the bike, the Hermit reasoned. From the looks of it, she had spent the entire night in the road.

What to do? thought the Hermit. *What to do?* The situation presented a moral dilemma far graver than that of a suitcase found in the road. The Hermit wasn't an indifferent person at heart, and the frail crumpled body on the ground in front of him didn't look very menacing. But experience had taught him to be wary of his fellow man.

She was still breathing—he could see that. There was a smudge of blood on her forehead where her head hit the rock. *What to do?* Surely someone would come along who was better qualified to care for her—a construction worker or delivery person, someone with paramedical skills or a pickup truck to take her to the hospital or home.

He took a few steps away. Although summer was over and most of the North Neck Road residents had gone home to Boston or New York for the season, there must be someone still living nearby.

But the sun wouldn't rise for another hour and the Chappy ferry wouldn't start running until 7 A.M. That would leave the woman out in the open for two more hours in the morning chill. She lay behind a bend in the road: suppose a car rounded the curve too quickly and ran over her before it could stop? The speed limit on North Neck Road—on all of Chappaquiddick—is twenty-five miles an hour. But a lot of vehicles, the Hermit knew, come barreling down the dirt road at forty.

The Hermit came back to the crumpled rag doll. Three times, he reached down to take her hand to feel for her pulse. Three times he pulled back. It had been more than a decade since the Hermit had touched or been touched by another human being. A word came into his mind now—*danger*—and every fiber in his being screamed for him to depart.

Finally, he picked up her hand. It felt limp—like a dead bird—its downy belly soft against the calluses of a man who spends much of his time outdoors, chopping wood, digging for shellfish, and removing fishhooks from biting bluefish. The whiteness of her skin stood out against his weathered palms.

The Hermit slid his sandpapery forefinger down her arm to take her pulse. Sure enough, he felt a faint flutter. But her hand felt cold and so did her forehead.

"Miss," he said, and his voice, unused for so long, sounded harsh and strange in his throat. "Miss." His voice rasped a little louder. No reaction. He brought his hand next to her cheek to shake her head or slap her. But the Hermit was afraid to hurt her.

You should call someone, the voice in his head said. But the Hermit had no phone. *You should find someone*, the voice said. But no one would be awake at this hour and besides, he didn't know the name of a single neighbor.

So he moved her bicycle to the side of the road and propped his fishing rod against it. He gathered the shawl around the woman's frail shoulders and wrapped the kerchief around her bald head. He took off his jacket and folded it around her, then picked her up in his arms and walked toward the ferry.

He walked back North Neck Road and passed the fork where Litchfield Road splits off from the main road. He walked past Caleb's Pond, the water shimmering in the silvery moonlight. He walked past Manaca Hill, where thanks to the dramatic harbor views, a simple one-story home sells for several million dollars. He walked past the Chappaquiddick Beach Club—its red, white, and blue cabanas immortalized in the movie *Jaws*.

She was a tiny thing. *Weighs less than a doe*, he thought as he strode through the morning mist. Like most of the locals, the Hermit hunted during the brief Chappaquiddick deer season, using a bow fashioned from local birch wood. The deer supplied him with venison jerky and venison bacon—both homemade— and much of the fresh meat he ate.

He was aware of the woman's shallow breathing, but he didn't quite dare to look at her face. He cradled her in his arms as gently as he could, his shoulders hunched to protect her from the wind. His torso began to ache, for even if she was light, he'd still carried a hundred pounds of dead weight for two miles. He should readjust her position, or set her down, but he didn't want to disturb her. So the Hermit continued walking without moving his upper body until they arrived at the ferry landing.

The sky had brightened from charcoal to lavender. Off in the distance, the façades of the white houses in Edgartown picked up the first golden glow of sunrise. A gull flew up and dropped a clam on the asphalt to crack the shell so it could peck out the mollusk hidden inside.

The sun would be up soon and perhaps he would see a jogger. The jogger would call the proper authorities on his cell phone. Someone qualified would assume charge of the woman's rescue, and the Hermit could return to his fishing.

But there were no joggers. Years ago, there had been a pay

phone in the shed by the ferry ramp, the Hermit remembered. But it seemed to be gone, and besides, he rarely carried money. So he sat down on the bench, cradled her in his arms to keep her warm, and waited for the ferry.

The first boat arrived a half hour later, bringing a landscaping crew and truck from the Verizon phone company. As the vehicles drove off, the Hermit walked up the ramp onto the ferry, the rag doll hugged to his chest.

Patrick did a double take at the sight of the Hermit emerging from the morning mist, the limp body of a woman draped across his arms.

"I found her on North Neck Road," he said to the ferry captain, and it was hard to say which of them—Patrick or the Hermit—was more surprised to hear his raspy voice. Again, the words sounded alien, almost metallic in the mouth of a man who didn't speak for months on end.

"I think she fell off her bicycle and hit her head on a rock," the Hermit said, his voice squeaking. "She's breathing. I didn't know who to call." *Good Lord, an entire monologue.* His scratchy voice dwindled to silence.

Patrick radioed the harbormaster, who radioed Sergeant Mayhew from the Edgartown Police Department. Patrick drove the ferry across the harbor with the Hermit still holding the woman in his arms.

They gently laid her down on a bench in the ferry office. Sergeant Mayhew arrived, then an ambulance, and the EMTs transferred her to a gurney. They hardly noticed the man with the wild hair and rough beard, and by the time someone thought to ask who brought her in, the Hermit had retreated to the shadows behind the Old Sculpin Gallery on Dock Street. He watched as the ambulance pulled away, then lingered awhile in Edgartown.

When the Hermit finally rode the ferry back to Chappaquiddick, Patrick refused to take his ticket.

"This one's on me," he said. "You know, you probably saved her life."

Then, reflecting on how uncharacteristically chatty the Hermit had been this morning, Patrick leaned over and said in the conspiratorial tone of one Martha's Vineyard fisherman to another: "Man, you should have seen the bluefish come through here an hour ago. They were jumping clear out of the water."

8

the hermit's lair

Claire unknotted the garbage bag and examined the coat. It had once been orange, but a decade of grime had darkened it to the shade of lampblack. It had once been slick and weatherproof, but harsh weather and wear had softened it like crumpled Kleenex. One pocket had come unstitched and hung like a limp handkerchief. The other was so full of seashells, twine, fishing lures, and an Opinel pen-knife, it bulged like a grapefruit. A tear zigzagged from collar to hem along the back; it had been clumsily mended with duct tape. In fact, the whole jacket had been darned and patched with fishing line so often, Claire could scarcely tell if the coat had originally been a parka, a slicker, or a jacket.

Claire's little bicycle escapade landed her in the Martha's Vineyard Hospital with a concussion and a sprained wrist. Mary Doheney drove down from Boston to help her daughter convalesce. Mary had Claire's slight build and delicate features, and like Claire, she favored sweater sets in muted colors. She still lived in the three-decker where Claire and her sisters had grown up.

"Claire Doheney, what on *earth* were you doing gallivanting on a bicycle in an isolated place like Chappaquiddick?" Mary said. She was knitting one of her famous afghans and her needles clicked with disapprobation. Mary Doheney believed one's hands should never be idle. "Apparently, you spent the whole night lying in the road," Mary said. "You're lucky you weren't killed."

Later that week, as Mary and Claire were leaving the hospital, one of the nurses came running out of the building with a plastic garbage bag. She reached to hand it to Claire. Mary leapt out of the car, intercepted the package, and shoved it in the trunk.

"What's that?" asked Claire.

"The man who found you wrapped you in his jacket. Let's just say it wasn't the cleanest garment." Mary had insisted on putting the jacket in the trunk of her car. She wouldn't hear of Claire hanging it in the Feinblat coat closet.

"The thing's probably crawling with fleas, ticks, and what have you," Mary said.

They compromised: Claire would store the jacket in the bike shed until she could return it to its rightful owner.

A smell emanated from the coat: a commingling of mustiness, sweat, and sea life. It had a rank feral quality, but after her initial repugnance, there was something appealing, too. It reminded Claire of the way one grew to appreciate a malodorous well-aged cheese.

Claire had been brought up to believe that the proper thing to do when someone lends you a jacket or sweater is to wash and fold it before returning it. She wasn't sure if her curious savior would appreciate the gesture—or even if the coat could survive laundering.

In the end, she brushed the pine needles off it with a whisk broom, folded it as neatly as she could, and put it in a paper shopping bag. The coat made her think of Molly.

Among the boyfriends Molly had brought home the previous spring was a biker and motorcycle mechanic named Wrench. The young man wore a denim jacket with white sweat circles where the arms had been cut off and jeans so stiff with grime, they could have stood upright when he took them off. Molly had dated Wrench off and on for several months, and as far as Claire could see, not once had he changed his clothes. Claire took to spraying Molly's room with Lysol whenever Wrench left after a visit.

Claire looked for her rescuer. He never showed up at the potluck suppers at the Chappy Community Center. She looked for him on the ferry, varying the times she crossed over to Edgartown. But he never boarded the boat when she did. She altered her route back and forth from the ferry, sometimes driving the long way, via Litchfield Road, making a large loop around the island. The man seemed to have disappeared.

One day, she asked Patrick about him.

"The Hermit?"

"Do you know where he lives?"

"I'm not sure anyone knows for certain where he lives," said Patrick. "I haven't exactly been invited to his house for dinner." He looked at Claire in an odd way. What on earth could she want with the Hermit?

Each time she saw Patrick, she asked about the mysterious man. He promised to do a little digging. One day, as she was coming back from the Breast Cancer Survivors Support Group, he waved a sheet of paper at her triumphantly. On the paper was a hand-sketched map of Chappaquiddick. He pointed to a wavy line running north just past the Chappy Store. It stretched from the main road to a small rectangle shaded with hash marks.

"This is the Chappy Cemetery," Patrick said, pointing to the rectangle. "The far side is flanked with woods. In the northeast corner, there's supposed to be an overgrown trail. At the end of that, there's supposed to be a smaller trail off to the right. Just before the end of that trail, look for a path—really more a deer track. I've never been there and neither has my informant."

Patrick paused theatrically and finished with a flourish: "And that is where you'll find the Hermit's lair."

"I didn't know there was a cemetery on Chappaquiddick," Claire said. She took the map and thanked him.

"Some of the most exclusive real estate on the island," said Patrick. He lowered his voice. "Hey, it's none of my business, Claire, but be careful. People talk. There's something strange about that guy and I don't think he wants company."

The next morning, as she did most days that fall, Claire set to work on the Reich manuscript. When Reich was twelve years old, his mother had an affair with his tutor. According to Ely, the young boy caught them in the act and alluded to the affair in front of his father. The elder Reich violently confronted Reich's mother. The woman committed a slow painful suicide by drinking a bottle of cleaning fluid.

"The poor child," Claire said sadly. "That must have haunted Reich his whole life."

Ely nodded. Feelings of guilt for his mother's death must have motivated Reich, at least in part, to enroll in medical school at the University of Vienna. Perhaps these painful feelings also led him to Sigmund Freud. Reich quickly became one of Freud's star students, and by the age of twenty-two, he was a practicing psychoanalyst in his own right.

Claire got up and brewed a fresh pot of coffee.

Reich became obsessed by Freud's theory of libido. The young psychoanalyst came to believe that this sexual energy was a literal physical force. His clinical work convinced him that most neuroses had their roots in sexual stasis, and that the key to a healthy life lay in what he called orgastic potency. In 1929, Reich wrote his first book, provocatively titled *The Function of the Orgasm.*

Here Claire sighed, for her own life certainly was in what Reich would have called an unhealthy state of sexual stasis. She felt so sullied by Harrison's infidelity and traumatized by her cancer treatments, she didn't have an ounce of sexual energy left in her.

Claire attempted to plunge into the next chapter, but her mind was elsewhere. She closed her computer and went to the kitchen to bake a loaf of cranberry nut bread. She roasted the walnuts in a skillet to give them a smoky flavor and perfumed the batter with cardamom and freshly grated orange zest. While the bread was cooling, she found a card, wrote a note, and tied it to the pan with raffia.

Here's what the note said:

Dear Neighbor,

I have looked for you everywhere. I wanted to thank you in person for the extraordinary assistance you gave me, a perfect stranger. I gather you found me in the road, carried me on foot to the ferry, and placed me in the care of the EMTs.

I'm back to normal now and I have decided to retire my bike as a shopping cart!

There aren't words enough to convey my deep gratitude. I hope you'll be pleased to know you probably saved my life.

I would welcome the opportunity to thank you in person. In the meantime, here's your jacket and a small token of my appreciation.

Claire Doheney

She placed the bread, pan, and note in the shopping bag. Then she drove past the Chappy Store—long since closed for the season. She turned left on the long dirt lane. It rose and fell, curved to the left, then the right, crossed a small creek, and passed some houses. It ended at a patch of neatly mown grass dotted with forty or fifty headstones. The spectacular views of the bay are the envy of every island developer. Thankfully, the land isn't for sale.

As Claire walked through the cemetery, she noticed a small square white marble headstone. LYDIA B., DAUGHTER OF BETSY AND GEORGE GARDNER, read the inscription. DIED OCTOBER 9, 1843, AT THE AGE OF 2 YEARS AND 9 MONTHS.

Claire shivered and raised her collar. The sky had turned dark and a northeast wind brought a cold drizzle. The last leaves had fallen from the trees. The bare bony branches stood silhouetted against the horizon.

She walked to the far corner of the cemetery. From a distance, the tree line looked unbroken, but as she approached, she saw, barely perceptible, a small path. She tucked her pant legs into her socks—a precaution against ticks—and ventured into the woods.

The trail, such as it was, continued for thirty yards. The farther it went, the more overgrown it became. Claire clambered over a fallen tree trunk. A few yards later, her foot sank to the ankle in a mud puddle that lay hidden under a pile of dead leaves. Mercifully there were no insects. *This place must be unbearable in the summertime*, Claire thought.

After fifteen minutes of slogging through the woods, Claire came to what seemed a dead end. A toppled beech tree barred the path. A dense thicket of underbrush blocked both sides. She searched for a way around these obstacles, but short of cutting a new path with a machete, there seemed no way to continue.

The rain fell steadily now, plastering the kerchief to her head. She wrapped the paper bag with the coat and cranberry bread in a plastic garbage bag she had thought to bring in case of bad weather. Discouraged, she turned to walk back toward the cemetery. A few yards back on the left, she spotted a faint trace of trail—more of a footpath. A large branch at chest height barred the entrance—that's why she hadn't noticed it earlier. As she bent to step under it, she noticed that the end of the branch looked to have been cut with an ax.

She continued a few dozen yards, brambles tearing at her pant legs. This trail, too, seemed to end in an impenetrable wall of forest. She rested her arm on the trunk of a scrub oak. Then she saw it. Behind the tree was another path and on that path, a muddy footprint made by a lug-soled boot.

Her heart beat faster. She ducked behind the tree onto this path and stepped over the footprint. She slipped and slid through the mud and leaves for another forty feet, then emerged into a clearing.

Every small island—no matter how exclusive or picturesque— has one. A junkyard where the residents bring the unlovely hulks of broken appliances, sagging sofas, three-legged tables, and wrecked cars. It starts as someone's personal rubbish pile and gradually becomes a communal dump. It serves that purpose until the property owner or an heir gets fed up and posts a NO TRESPASSING sign. Then another dump springs up somewhere else, and the process begins anew.

Claire stood in such a spot now. To her left was an old-fashioned washing machine, its wringers jammed with branches. To the right, an eviscerated icebox and an old coal-burning stove, door dangling from a broken hinge. A harrow with rusted blades trailed behind an old tractor missing its engine. Behind them, the moldering carcasses of an old Woody and a '54 Dodge. Off to the side stood a newer vehicle—a BMW convertible. A pine tree grew through its floorboards; its canvas top hung in shreds.

Behind the junkyard stood a house, or more precisely, the

wreckage of what had once been a house. The roof of the rear porch had collapsed into a pile of rotted shingles. Moss, ferns, and waist-high saplings carpeted what was visible of the remaining roof. Once there had been an entryway, but the support pilings had long since rotted and the landing hung at a 60-degree angle. Two windows flanked the door, their panes broken or missing. An air of Dickensian decrepitude hung about the structure. Had Edgar Allan Poe lived on Chappaquiddick, this would have been his House of Usher.

Claire took a step forward and tripped over something. She looked down. The eye sockets of a yellowed skull stared back at her. Its long stained teeth were clenched in a ghastly grimace. A few feet in front of her was another skull, then another, then a sun-bleached spine and rib cage. The ground around her was littered with bones—of rabbits, birds, and deer.

A few years ago, a literary agent had brought Claire a proposal for a biography of the Cambodian dictator, Pol Pot. She read a few chapters, but when she got to an account of Cambodia's killing fields, she threw down the manuscript in disgust.

"I try to publish books about people who have added some measure of good to the world," she explained to the agent. The gruesome descriptions of the Khmer Rouge butchery gave Claire nightmares for weeks.

The vision of the killing fields returned, and Claire Doheney now found herself standing among them on Chappaquiddick. She took a step back, and a rabbit rib cage crunched under her shoe. She shrieked in horror, dropped the bag with the jacket, and ran as fast as her legs would carry her down the path back to the cemetery.

9

a singular courtship

There ensued a singular "courtship." You could call it a courtship, at least, for want of a better word. It was more than a series of random acts of kindness, but less than an actual relationship. It was certainly singular, as its participants neither courted nor spoke. They had, in fact, never consciously met.

A few days after Claire dropped the Hermit's coat and the cranberry bread in the junkyard behind the cemetery, the same shopping bag—a little the worse for wear—appeared next to the Feinblat mailbox on North Neck Road. In it was Claire's pan, filled with what appeared to be a loaf of nut bread. The loaf gave off a musky aroma whose origin Claire couldn't quite place.

Well I'll be damned, Claire thought. *The Hermit knows how to cook.*

The following week, Claire canned some rose hip preserves. She put a couple of jars in the shopping bag and returned to the path off the cemetery. She couldn't quite bring herself to venture as far as the bone yard, so she hung the bag from a protruding branch where she figured the Hermit would find it.

A few days later, the bag reappeared—this time with a couple of old peanut butter jars filled with a dark crimson jelly. Claire unscrewed the lid of one and sniffed. The smell was at once familiar and exotic. *Beach plum jam*? She tasted a little at the end of a breadstick and licked her lips with pleasure.

Not long after that, Claire hung the shopping bag—now patched all over with duct tape—at what both parties had tacitly come to consider the Hermit's drop spot. In it was an apple pie with an intricate lattice top.

Claire found herself impatiently awaiting the rounds of the Chappaquiddick mail lady—her excuse to walk to the mailbox. Sure enough: a couple days later, both bag and pie pan were returned—the latter now filled with a fragrant hazelnut pear tart.

The following week, Claire sent over a plate of her chocolate ricotta brownies—highly prized among her friends and authors. To give credit where due, this creation wasn't solely Claire's. The recipe came from the Italian bakery where Mary Doheney worked in Boston's North End.

Had the participants in this little ritual been asked what they thought they were doing, each would have answered that he or she was simply reciprocating an unexpected kindness from an unknown neighbor.

Had Elliott weighed in on their psychological motives, he would have pointed out Claire's obvious gratitude to the man who saved her life. He might also have cited her less immediately obvious urge to recover some of her maternal instincts after the operation—a procedure viewed by many women as an attack on the primal source of nurturing. In any case, he would have been pleased by what he would have called Claire's return from the exile of illness to the hopeful realm of health.

He didn't know the Hermit's motives, of course, but he might have speculated on the practice of gift giving among primitive peoples.

As for what Reich would have thought, well, the practitioner of what by 1935 he termed *character analytic vegetotherapy* would have focused on the strength of their respective sexual energies. In this, he would have found both parties sorely deficient.

Yet this strange exchange of food was more than just an alimentary tit for tat. It was nothing less than a dialogue— phrased in flavor and spoken in spice—with an eloquence worthy of a conversation in an eighteenth-century French salon.

One of the participants gave thanks for being alive. The other, after so many years of solitude, took some small pleasure in cooking for someone else.

For these weren't ordinary apple pies or nut breads. No.

To make the pie, Claire drove to a farm in Chilmark to buy the right ratio of sweet-tart Macoun and Cortland apples to mild aromatic McIntoshes. It goes without saying that she made the crust by hand—with stone-ground wheat flour and organic butter. Then, in a stroke of inspiration, and mindful of an old New England adage—"Apple pie without the cheese / Is like a kiss without the squeeze"—she enriched the dough with some grated Vermont sharp cheddar.

As for the nut bread, the Hermit made it with fresh hazelnuts shucked from beak-shaped pods picked off trees that grow in the woods on Sampson's Hill. He had ground the "flour" by hand from roasted acorns from Chappaquiddick oak trees. Not that Claire would have recognized the latter, for two centuries had passed since New Englanders routinely used acorn flour in place of what at the time had been hard-to-grow wheat.

If either Claire or the Hermit bothered to make preserves, the fruit would, of course, be local and hand harvested. Earlier that fall, Claire had gone to the Chappy Point Beach to gather the bulbous red sepals of *Rosa canina*, more commonly known as rose hips. Although not an indigenous species, the beach rose grows in profusion on the backshores of Chappaquiddick beaches. According to Dr. Gupta, the tart red fruit contains prodigious doses of antioxidants, which are effective in preventing infections.

Around the same time, and unbeknownst to Claire, the Hermit prowled nearly the same littoral zones in search of the tart, dark purple, olive-shaped fruit of *Prunus maritima*. Better know as the beach plum, this plant is indigenous to Martha's Vineyard and Cape Cod and requires equal patience and perseverance to procure.

Given that it takes several buckets of either fruit to produce a few modest pints of preserves, most people would have considered Claire's and the Hermit's foraging efforts extravagant if not downright crazy. To Claire and the Hermit, one slather of the fragrant preserves on a hot slice of toast made the hours of foraging and cooking worth the trouble.

These food gifts were edible declarations of friendship—a statement, by the way, that their authors would have denied vehemently. They were made by two people who loved to cook, but whose circumstances had deprived them of people to cook for.

Perhaps there was even some showboating. Both Claire and the Hermit were great cooks, instinctive cooks—the sort who add to each dish they make, not only the best possible ingredients, but a little piece of their souls. Each sensed in the other an audience worthy of his talents.

In any courtship—even the unspoken kind—there comes a point of escalation. One party makes a gesture intended to move the relationship to another level. It might be as simple

as reaching for a hand or bending down for a kiss, or as suggestive as inviting the other party up to one's apartment for a
nightcap.

In this peculiar relationship the escalation came in a small
white envelope taped to the plate with the brownies.

Here's what the note inside said:

My Culinary Friend:

*We haven't had the pleasure of meeting, but I'd like to
invite you to join me and some friends for Thanksgiving
dinner.*

*There's no need to dress up and you certainly don't
need to bring anything. Dinner will start around six p.m.*

*I hope you can make it. It would mean a lot to me
if you came.*

Claire

*P.S. My friends are the Feinblats—they own the house
where I'm staying. They love food as much as we do and
they're really nice.*

The postscript was added almost apologetically, as though
Claire sensed how apprehensive the Hermit might be about
crowds.

"You invited the Hermit?" asked Sheila, incredulous.

"He's nice," said Claire. "At least, I think he's nice. Well,
I've never really met him."

"As my grandfather used to say, 'Everyone is welcome under my tent,'" Sheila said. "Annabel will have a field day."

She told Claire about Annabel's latest exercise in good Sa-
maritanism. The little girl had spearheaded a food drive at her
elementary school, then managed to persuade the administration to set up a kiosk where homeless people could come twice
a week for sandwiches.

"Just what you well-heeled Upper East Siders had in mind

when you forked over tuition for private school," Claire said. The women had a good laugh.

One person was not laughing, however: the recipient of Claire's invitation.

It had been a long time—more than a decade—since anyone had invited the Hermit anywhere. How would he dress? What would he say? How could he tolerate being in a closed space with other people?

It would mean a lot to me if you came.

He read the last line of Claire's note over and over. The sad fact was, it had been so long since the Hermit had had a Thanksgiving dinner with other people, he didn't even know what date the holiday fell on this year.

This time, when Claire got back the tattered shopping bag, there was no reciprocal food gift. Instead, she found a small note written with a fountain pen.

Thank you, it said. *I'll try.*

10

giving thanks

T oday we are giving thanks," Elliott said, raising his glass of Gevrey-Chambertin.

"For new friends." Here he nodded to Ely and the surprise guest, Wrench.

"For great food." Here he glanced at everyone at the table, for all had contributed in some way to the splendid feast before them.

"And above all, for good health," said Elliott. Everyone turned to Claire, who the previous week had completed her final round of chemotherapy. She smiled and tipped her head gratefully.

"Amen!" said Sheila. All clinked glasses and sipped the wine.

And what wine it was! Wrench's eyes grew round as bottle bottoms. The biker had guzzled a lot of wine in his day, but nothing he had ever tasted—or could even imagine—prepared him for the complexity and finesse of the burgundy Elliott had unearthed from his wine cellar to accompany Thanksgiving dinner.

Observing the young man's wonderment—or perhaps just pained by his awkward grip on the glass—Elliott leaned over and asked Wrench if he would like to learn the proper way to taste wine.

The biker nodded his head like a bobble doll.

So Elliott taught Wrench the correct way to hold the wineglass (by the stem, not the bowl), how to sniff the wine before tasting it (plunge your nose into the bowl, but don't let your face touch the rim), and how to take a small sip, swirl it around your mouth, and aerate it before swallowing.

This Wrench did, and the wine's extraordinary cedar-leather-blackberry scents exploded in olfactory Technicolor. He took a sip, drawing in air, as Elliott had showed him, and the wine's complex flavor components seemed to ricochet in his mouth like buckshot.

"Forty percent of what you taste in a wine is actually smell," explained Elliott, and he launched into a dissertation on the role of retronasal sinus activity in wine appreciation. Wrench was shocked to learn that there are wine experts who actually spit the stuff out after tasting it.

"Shiiiiit," he said with admiration.

Mary Doheney shot him a look that said: *Watch your language, young man. And mind how much you drink.*

Molly shot him a look that said: *Stop being such a candy ass.*

Meanwhile, a similar outburst of gustatory pleasure took place at the other end of the table. Ely had just eaten a forkful of oat bran stuffing with oyster essence. His eyebrows rose and his eyes half closed in the beatific look one observes in Fra Angelico frescoes. Sheila placed a slice of smoked turkey onto his plate and Claire filled the wineglass he had previously covered with the palm of his hand.

"You're trying to corrupt me," said Ely.

"Who, me?" said Sheila. She gave him a conspiratorial wink.

Ely had shelved his sauerkraut diet a few weeks earlier. The fledgling biographer now subsisted on a Spartan regimen of oat bran.

"How do you eat it?" Sheila had asked.

"With water," said Ely.

"No one's going to eat a bowl of oat bran with water at this Thanksgiving table," Sheila said. Claire agreed. Ely watched helplessly as Claire sautéed some oat bran with onions, celery, currants, and pine nuts. She added some turkey stock and oyster juices—left over from the oyster stuffing—to make a sort of pilaf.

Ely had been expected for the holiday dinner, as were Molly and Mary Doheney. Wrench's attendance came as a surprise. Claire made it clear after the last boyfriend Molly had brought to Chappaquiddick that the girl was to visit alone.

So when Wrench's Harley Fat Boy roared up the driveway, with sawn-off tailpipes and Molly perched on the back, it made a less-than-favorable first impression. Claire had been editing, Mary knitting, Elliott reading, and Sheila checking emails. All were jolted out of these peaceful activities by the squeal of tires on the scallop shell driveway and a backfire that resounded like a gunshot.

To Wrench's credit and in respect for the holiday, the biker had finally changed his clothes. However, the image on the back of his new black leather motorcycle jacket depicted a couple engaged in oral sex. Elliott frowned and Sheila reddened. Mary rushed to explain to the clueless Wrench that this was not, perhaps, the most appropriate insignia to wear when visiting a home with small children.

Claire gave Molly a dirty look, to which the latter replied with a shrug. Sunlight glinted off the strips of aluminum foil and electrical wire she had braided into her hair.

Then Wrench did three things that were totally out of character for Molly's boyfriends.

He reached in the Harley's saddlebags and produced flower bouquets for Claire and Sheila.

He addressed his hosts as "Mr. and Mrs. Feinblat" ("Dr. Feinblat," Claire softly corrected) and extended his hand (fingers tattooed with the letters R I D E F R E E) to shake the doctor's hand.

And he wiped his feet on the doormat and took off his motorcycle boots before entering the cottage.

Molly blasted him with a glare of pure contempt.

Ever the preemptor, Mary Doheney took control of the situation. The offending jacket was hung in the bike shed that once housed the Hermit's coat. Molly and Wrench were shown to separate bedrooms, one on either side of Mary's. One look from the grandmother made it clear that nocturnal fraternization would not be tolerated.

Later that afternoon, Wrench watched Elliott struggle to change the propane tank on his dual-fuel barbecue grill and smoker. Two months of disuse and salty sea air had frozen the locknut solid. Wrench produced Vise-Grip pliers from one of the Fat Boy's saddlebags. He loosened the coupling and switched the tank in a matter of seconds.

"What does your furnace run on?" Wrench asked Elliott. The doctor replied uncertainly he supposed it was propane.

"Then you must have an underground tank somewhere," Wrench said. "Why don't we hook up your grill to it so you won't have to swap out propane cylinders every few weeks?"

Fifteen minutes later, Wrench had located a thousand-gallon propane tank buried behind the garage. Two hours later, he had ridden to Edgartown Hardware, purchased the necessary valves, pipes, and couplings, and connected the grill to the underground tank. By the end of the day, the enterprising Wrench had changed the filters on the Feinblat furnace, replaced the antifreeze in Claire's SUV, and programmed Sheila's TiVo.

"I like this kid," Elliott told Claire.

Nate followed Wrench around like a puppy dog. "Can I ride on the Harley?" he asked. "*Please*, can I ride on the Harley?"

Wrench came to Elliott's rescue before the doctor even had to invent an excuse. "Maybe in a couple years, Nate. You and your sister are too young to ride on a motorcycle now."

"I really like this kid," Elliott said.

"Brownnoser," Molly hissed. She gave Wrench a withering scowl.

The next morning, Claire and Ely disappeared into Claire's office to work on the Reich manuscript. They emerged at noon to help Mary and Annabel set the table.

Claire casually asked them to set an extra place.

"For whom?" Mary asked. Sheila shot Claire a sly look.

"Oh, no one special," Claire said nonchalantly. "The man who rescued me after the bike accident."

"You invited the Hermit?" Mary asked, and it was unclear what registered louder in her voice: incredulity or alarm.

"I wonder if he got any of our groceries," said Annabel, who had brought a box of canned food from New York to donate to the Martha's Vineyard Food Bank.

"Have you met him?" asked Mary.

"We've been swapping messages," said Claire. "Well, not really messages. Food. A fruit pie. A jar of preserves. Sort of like notes in a bottle. Don't worry—he probably won't come."

Claire seemed atypically cheerful that afternoon as they busied themselves in the kitchen. When she went upstairs to shower and dress for dinner, Sheila noticed she had put on makeup—just a little—and perfume. Claire hadn't worn perfume since the Valentine's Day Harrison left her.

At 6 P.M., Elliott made the house cocktail—Katama Kirs—which consisted of vintage champagne and blueberry syrup.

By seven, everyone had moved to the dining room table. The Hermit looked to be a no-show.

And what a dinner it was—a meal worthy of Elliott's lofty epicurean standards. Chestnuts roasted in an antique long-handled skillet in the fireplace accompanied the blueberry Kirs. Sheila made chopped turkey liver pâté to serve with Mary Doheney's Irish soda bread. Claire ladled out a Hubbard squash bisque sprinkled with chili-crusted *pepitas*.

The main course featured turkey from a farm in West Tisbury—organic, free range, and freshly slaughtered, it goes without saying—which Elliott had brined with bourbon and maple syrup the previous day and smoked over smoldering maple wood. The process was a lot easier now that Wrench had connected the grill and smoker to the underground propane tank.

The stuffing combined Claire's freshly baked corn bread with briny oysters from Katama Bay. Nate and Annabel helped arrange artisanal marshmallows on top of the sweet potato casserole. Even Molly stopped sulking long enough to join her mother in concocting an astringent cranberry-kumquat relish.

That left just two people not directly involved with the cooking: Wrench and Ely. Wrench's culinary skills were pretty much limited to transferring the contents of cans to plastic bowls for the microwave. But he claimed to have a recipe for a great "cheap date hash," which he promised to make for breakfast. Ely offered to help, but Sheila had had enough oat bran for one meal. She shooed him out of the kitchen.

Naturally, the talk at the dinner table soon turned to publishing. Elliott had just completed a successful book tour in Australia. *It's Your Responsibility* was entering its ninth week at the top of the *Sydney Morning Herald* bestseller list. Sheila was working on a sequel to *Miss Millipede*, and Claire was up to her eyeballs in the Reich manuscript.

She turned to Ely to continue a conversation they had started that morning. "So when the International Psychoanalytic Association expelled Reich in 1934, they actually did him a favor?"

"Who's Reich?" Wrench asked.

"The reason my mother's nose is always buried in a manuscript," Molly muttered.

"Well, they certainly freed him from the restraints of traditional psychoanalysis," Ely said. "Especially the taboo against physical contact with the patient."

"You mean shrinks get to touch, not just talk?" Wrench asked. Mary gave him a look that said: *Watch it.*

"Not normally," Ely said. "The goal of traditional psychoanalysis is to recover painful memories that have been repressed in the subconscious. Reich believed it wasn't enough simply to verbalize these memories. You have to express them in a burst of energy and emotion."

Ely bounced in his seat with excitement.

"Traditional analysts encouraged the free association of ideas and memories," he said. "Dr. Reich focused on a patient's breathing—and more precisely, where the respiration was blocked. 'Breathing is like free-associating,' he would say."

Here Wrench took a long deep breath. Everyone laughed. By now the whole table was listening.

"Most psychoanalysts at the time sat behind the couch out of sight so as not to distract the patient from free-associating," Ely continued. "Reich would set his chair close so he could watch the patient's posture and facial expressions. He would ask his patients to strip to their underwear during therapy sessions, so he could observe their 'musculature armoring'— the emotional blocks in their bodies. Deadness in the face and the eyes, for example, was a way to avoid crying. Perpetually hunched shoulders suggested crushing painful feelings.

Tightness in the jaw and throat indicated someone who 'choked down' his anger. The therapist's job, Reich believed, was to help the emotions break through the body's armor."

Molly perked up momentarily.

"So Reich would touch the patient—press hard with his thumb on the jaw or lay his hand on the chest to help release a pent-up outburst of crying. He'd put his face right in front of a patient's and make frightening grimaces to try to help break through the emotional mask."

Here Ely made a scary face at Annabel, who shrieked with delight.

"Sounds sadistic," said Elliott.

"It had the potential to be sadistic, and many of Reich's followers, if not quite sadistic, became unpleasantly doctrinaire. But I always found that Reich approached his therapy sessions with warmth and a sense of humor," Ely said.

"You knew Reich personally?" Wrench asked, his eyes again as round as coasters.

"Yes, I did," said Ely, "and let me tell you, he could really bring out your emotions."

"Those personal recollections are what's going to make Ely's biography so compelling," Claire said.

Another admiring *"shiiiiit"* formed on Wrench's lips, but Mary cut him short. Molly gave him a bored yawn and motioned for them to leave the table.

But Wrench had never experienced a conversation like this. "These people are *so* smart," he whispered. He wasn't about to miss a syllable.

Besides, Elliott was uncorking another bottle—this time, a dessert wine. It wasn't every day that a Harley-riding hellion got the opportunity to taste a Trockenbeerenauslese from the Mosel. Elliott explained how two or three times a decade, when the harvest is late and weather conditions are right, the grapes are attacked by a benevolent fungus called *botrytis*. This "noble rot," as the fungus is called, causes the grapes to shrivel on the vine, concentrating their flavor and sweetness.

Wrench twirled his glass, as Elliott had shown him, admiring how the wine's syrupy "legs" descended in a languorous trickle. He deeply inhaled a perfume suggestive of honey, almonds, and apricots—the latter, explained Elliott, the telltale sign of botrytis. Elliott was right: Wine was a living thing and its character seemed to develop with each passing minute it sat in the glass.

Dessert was an apotheosis of pumpkin. Claire made pumpkin pie with pumpkin ice cream. Sheila dished up a New York deli–style pumpkin cheesecake. Mary produced a platter of pumpkin "blondies." Claire showed Annabel and Nate how to grate fresh nutmeg using a miniature silver grater she had acquired in Paris. The children discharged this duty with such enthusiasm, the adults came to wonder whether they were eating pumpkin pie with nutmeg or nutmeg with pumpkin pie.

"I'm sorry your friend didn't show," Sheila said later that evening.

She and Claire were rinsing the dishes and loading them into the dishwasher. Nate and Annabel brought the several dozen empty wineglasses from the table and lined them up on the black granite counter. Wrench had gone outside with Elliott to help clean the grill. Elliott was tempted to introduce the young man to Cuban cigars, but reflected that one vice was enough for the evening. Ely had gone off to work on his manuscript, and Mary had decided to have a little attitude-adjusting chat with Molly.

Claire tried to make light of it—maybe he had other plans for the holiday.

"He's a hermit," said Sheila with sympathy. "Maybe hermits don't do holiday dinners."

"Well, it's not like I called to invite him," said Claire. "I don't even know his name."

The next morning, the silence of North Neck Road was shattered by the screams and thumps of Ely's bioenergetic exercises. Or more accurately, by two sets of screams and thumps. The previous evening, Claire had warned everyone about Ely's morning ritual. The ever-inquisitive Wrench had asked if he could watch. To judge from the sound of the screaming duet, Ely now had a disciple.

A half hour later, Wrench reported for duty in the kitchen. Soon chopped onions, diced turkey, peeled chestnuts, and leftover oyster stuffing were sizzling away in a large cast-iron skillet. To this mixture, the biker added a quarter of a can of black pepper and half a bottle of Tabasco sauce.

"Why is it called 'cheap date hash'?" asked Nate.

"Because you make it the morning after with the leftovers from your girlfriend's dinner," explained Wrench.

"The morning after what?" asked Nate.

Wrench looked to Elliott for help, but the latter sipped his coffee without comment. He cocked his finger as if to say, *It's your responsibility.*

Wrench gulped.

Despite the eclectic nature of the ingredients—or perhaps on account of it—the hash was pronounced outstanding, even if the hot sauce sent Mary lunging for a glass of milk. Ely looked up from his bowl of oat bran and cold water. Dr. Reich would have seen envy and misery in his facial expression. Sheila took the bowl away from him and put down a plate of cheap date hash.

"It's our secret, Ely," she said with a smile.

When, finally, it came time for everyone to leave Sunday morning, Sheila and Claire stood on the porch.

"It was a nice weekend," Claire said.

Ely agreed and folded himself back into his Volkswagen. Mary agreed and wedged herself in the car amid the boxes of manuscript. Ely would drop her off in Boston on his way back to Maine. Sheila handed him a paper bag: Ely had forgotten his oat bran.

Elliott asked Wrench when his birthday was and disappeared in the cellar. He reemerged a few minutes later with a bottle of 1988 Château Léoville-Las Cases.

"Drink this on your birthday," Elliot said. "You were born in a spectacular year for Bordeaux."

Much to Elliott's surprise, Wrench had something for him, too: a maintenance schedule. The young man had examined every system in the North Neck house—electrical, plumbing, heating, air-conditioning, gas—and he wrote out a complete list of what needed to be checked and changed when.

In fact, only one person was *not* sorry to leave the holiday gathering on Chappaquiddick.

Molly could tolerate a lot of shortcomings in the men she dated, but Wrench had crossed the line.

He had, it seemed, committed the unpardonable sin of making a favorable impression on the grown-ups.

11

how many shrinks?

The Hermit dipped his peep box in the water. The sea bottom came into view and with it, the delicately crenellated shell of a bay scallop. The Hermit stood in hip waders in water up to his waist amid waving clumps of eelgrass. He was one of a handful of fishermen doing a time-honored activity that takes place on Martha's Vineyard every year from November to March. He was bay scalloping in Shear Pond.

As it turned out, there were *two* people who were less than thrilled by the Feinblat–Doheney Thanksgiving weekend.

The first was Molly, whose plan for bringing the controversial Wrench to dinner had completely and abysmally backfired.

The second was the Hermit, who, technically, wasn't a no-show at all.

Had Molly been asked how she felt about the holiday

weekend, she surely would have said pissed off. Why endure a bone-jarring five-hour ride from New York on the back of a noisy Harley-Davidson if you can't cause a little mayhem? Why bring a bona fide biker with porn on the back of his jacket if you can't aggravate your mom and her intellectual friends?

Had the moon been shining the night of Thanksgiving and had Claire looked outside, she might have seen a raggedy man lurking in the shadows. Had Claire explored the Feinblat backyard the morning after Thanksgiving, she might have found a footprint or two from a lug boot bearing a suspicious resemblance to the print she saw on the path behind the Chappaquiddick Cemetery.

But Claire stayed indoors that Friday morning. Her mind was elsewhere. She was busy writing a letter.

A peep box is a wooden box or bucket with a pane of glass at the bottom. It works on the same principle as swim goggles. It allows you to get a clear view underwater without getting your head wet. When the tan, gray, or black shell of a bay scallop comes into sight, you scoop it up with a dip net, a long pole with a mesh bag attached at one end.

Most of the professional scallopers on Martha's Vineyard use dredges pulled by power boats, but a few of the old-timers still harvest scallops with a peep box and dip net. Especially in Shear Pond, a shallow inlet at the end of Cape Poge where, centuries ago, colonists would wash the sheep pastured on Chappaquiddick for the summer in preparation for shearing. If a guy knows what he's doing, he can bring in a bushel in a half hour. With bay scallops retailing for upwards of twenty dollars a pound, it's a decent way to earn some extra cash in the winter. The Hermit scalloped for his own consumption, and while normally he was a proficient fisherman, this morning his heart wasn't in it.

Had Elliott weighed in on Molly's motives, he might have

called her behavior a cry for attention. Then again, since he was Molly's godfather and had watched her grow up, he was hardly an impartial observer. He was almost as inept at reading her motives as was the person closest to her: Claire.

Had Reich seen Molly, he would immediately have detected anger. A hot self-absorbed rage that boiled from her eyes, locked her jaw, puffed out her chest, and emanated from her defiantly set pelvis.

The Hermit's feelings were more complex. Claire's invitation had left him feeling both flattered and threatened. Flattered, because after all these years of isolation, someone had actually invited him to a holiday dinner. Not only that, but said someone knew how to handle herself in the kitchen. In his own way, the Hermit was a food snob—he cared as deeply about what he ate as a Manhattan foodie like Elliott.

He also flattered himself because he had made an uncharacteristic decision and taken an atypical risk and both had worked out. He had helped a stranger in need—taken a helpless woman under his wing, as it were—and she actually repaid him in kindness. It was not currency the Hermit normally received and it made him feel strangely affluent.

Bay scallops are one of Martha's Vineyard's best-kept secrets. Nantucket bay scallops get all the press, but Vineyard scallops are every bit as sweet—aficionados would say even sweeter. As a recreational fisherman, the Hermit was entitled to a bushel of bay scallops a week. Of course, living by himself, he needed considerably less than the limit—even if he ate scallops every day of the season.

If the Hermit felt flattered by the invitation to Thanksgiving dinner, he also felt threatened. Attending would have meant forsaking the safety of his solitude for an evening. Solitude was his main defense against the cruelty and ridicule of other people, and the Hermit had had a bellyful of both. With regards to cruelty, even the Hermit knew he was being a bit paranoid. It was unlikely that this wisp of a woman, who lived by herself on North Neck Road, would ever be in a position to hurt him.

As for ridicule, it was a very real risk, which the Hermit, in the way of one of the Chinese warrior-philosophers he liked to read, had contrived to turn into a weapon. The Hermit wasn't poor: he certainly could afford new clothes or a haircut. But early on, he had noticed how his unruly hair and rumpled garments repelled other people—especially the summer folk. The worse he looked, the less people bothered him. By fully embracing the persona of a hermit, he had made himself virtually invisible. To paraphrase the warrior-philosopher, "Sometimes the best defense is to be offensive."

As the Hermit made his way to the cottage on North Neck Road, flattery and fear warred within him. Flattery got him as far as the Feinblat driveway. Fear kept him from knocking on the door. He peeked through the windows and saw happy well-dressed people drinking wine, eating hors d'oeuvres, and making small talk by the warmth of the fire. All at once, he saw himself for what he really was—an awkward ungainly misfit. He no more belonged at that Thanksgiving table than would a wild beast. He retreated to the shadow of the woods and observed the warmth and amiability he wasn't a part of for a bit longer. Then he hunched his shoulders and in his loping gait retraced his steps and returned home.

Had Elliott met the Hermit that night, his first concern would not have been psychotherapeutic. As a certain best-selling self-help book explains, if you see someone begging or homeless, your first duty is to make sure he doesn't go hungry. The moment Claire invited the Hermit, Elliott pledged his hospitality—and he would have been the first to fill his guest's plate and top off his glass. But to tell the truth, Elliott was secretly relieved that the Hermit was a no-show. The presence of a stranger would have changed the social dynamics. Besides, his supply of '74 Gevrey-Chambertin was limited.

For Reich, the Hermit would have represented a classic case study in emotional armoring. His whole being—the vague gaze, expressionless face, hunched shoulders, and off-putting outfit—projected a need to block out painful feelings and social contact. The same was true for the rubbish in front of his house. Reich loved challenging cases on which he could test his new theories. With someone like the Hermit as a patient, the doctor would have had a field day.

Molly hadn't always been angry. A photo on Claire's desk showed Molly on her first day of first grade, her long straight hair tied neatly with a bright red bow, her face open and her smile incandescent. Claire would bring Molly to book signings with her authors. No matter how highfalutin the company or how intellectual the conversation, Molly always seemed to fit in.

Molly took to her various au pairs with characteristic warmth and openness. No matter where they came from—Olga from Belarus, Paola from Brazil, Minnie from Barbados—each found a place in the little girl's heart.

Molly's favorite au pair was a twenty-two-year-old graduate from the University of Helsinki. Annikki had high cheekbones and blond ringlet curls that cascaded down her shoulders. Her pale blue eyes crinkled when she laughed, which she did as often as possible. Annikki stood six feet tall in her bare feet, which made her a giant next to Molly and Mommy. Even Daddy had to raise his head when he spoke to her.

It was Annikki who initiated Molly into the feminine arts of makeup and hairstyling. She taught Molly how to gloss her lips and rouge her cheeks with a dab of lipstick. Each morning, she made an elaborate ritual of brushing and braiding Molly's hair. For her part, Molly would watch, spellbound, as Annikki curled her ringlets with Hot Rollers, applying gels and mousses just so to make her hair shine like sunlight.

If Claire thought that Annikki primped a little too much, she kept her opinion to herself. Claire knew she wasn't what you called a girlie-girl. Maybe it wouldn't hurt for Molly to learn a few beauty skills from this surrogate older sister from Finland.

There was another photo of Molly on Claire's desk, taken when Molly was thirteen. Her eyes are dark. Her mouth is sullen. And already she has started with the bizarre hairdos. Throughout her teenage years, Molly subjected her hair to every imaginable outrage. One day it would be orange. The next month green. Or yellow, crimson, or indigo. Over the years, she had sported a shag, a mullet, a crew cut, a Mohawk. When Molly was fifteen, she grew dreadlocks and didn't wash her hair for six months.

"You have such pretty hair, Molly," her grandmother Mary would say. "Why do you treat it so badly?"

Just when they thought her hair couldn't get any worse, Molly shaved her head. Then she let one side grow out and kept the other side shaved. But even these looked winsome compared to the time she grew her hair long again, then singed it with a blowtorch. She hoped the crinkly charred edges would give her what she perversely called "burn victim chic."

Her grades were equally erratic. "Highly intelligent, but doesn't apply herself," read the typical teacher's comment on her report cards. Molly would slide by doing as little homework as possible for three months, then turn in a brilliant term paper on a topic like "Structure and Chaos in *Anna Karenina*." When it came time for college applications, Claire hired a tutor to help Molly prepare for her SATs. She and the tutor spent the study time getting stoned. The night before the exam, she stayed out at a punk rock bar in the Bowery until 4 A.M. But when the results were mailed home a month later, Molly received a near perfect score in verbal and a 722 in math.

Elliott suggested therapy sessions and offered to put Molly on Prozac.

"She'll grow out of it," Mary reassured Claire. After all, hadn't she, Claire, been something of a hellion herself?

Wrench turned out to be such a pleasant surprise, Claire forgot to be angry with Molly for bringing him. Claire forgot to be angry a lot these days—especially since she'd finished her last round of chemotherapy. Claire had been so bitter and so angry for so long—about her cancer, about Harrison, about Beidermann—she didn't have a lot of negative emotions left in her. Her months in treatment had turned her anger into something unexpected: gratitude for being alive.

The letter Claire wrote when her mind was elsewhere was addressed to the Thanksgiving no-show. Here's how it read:

Dear Friend,

I am sorry about Thanksgiving. It strikes me I was inconsiderate.

I hoped to show you off to my friends, make you part of our holiday dinner, and yes, I'll admit it, to impress you with our cooking. I wanted to repay your culinary largesse all these weeks. And I still want to thank in person the man who saved my life.

It didn't occur to me to take your desire for privacy into consideration. I did not stop to think whether you might want to meet me or my friends. Please don't think ill of me—I meant no offense.

So I humbly extend another invitation. Dinner for two here on North Neck Road. A week from today at 8 p.m. Just you and me—no fanfare or friends. There's no need to reply. I'll set the table and make dinner for both of us. If you come, I will be delighted, but I'll understand if you don't. This will be the last invitation.

Claire

One day when Molly was twelve, she stayed home from school with a sprained ankle. Annikki put her to bed early. The two girls got under the covers and watched Annikki's favorite American movie, *Dirty Dancing*. Molly must have dozed off, for when she awoke, Annikki was gone and her bedroom was dark. Mommy had to work late that night, so Molly limped down the hall past Daddy's office to Annikki's room.

When Molly opened Annikki's door, there were Annikki and Daddy. Annikki sat on the bed, her blouse unbuttoned to the waist. Daddy stood in front of her. Daddy ran his fingers through Annikki's hair—the blond ringlets shimmered like spun gold in the lamplight. A moment later, Daddy made a funny noise and his body seemed to shake like Jell-O. Daddy didn't see Molly, but Annikki did. The surrogate big sister gave Molly a scowl that let her know she shouldn't say anything about what she saw to Claire or anyone else.

Molly hobbled back to her room and looked at her own hair in the mirror. It was dark, straight, and hopelessly limp. She tried, without success, to twirl it into curls with her fingers. She wished she could cut it all off.

Molly never told Claire about Annikki. Or the other au pairs and students and teaching assistants she'd see Daddy with on other occasions. Why bother? She could always torture her hair in some bizarre new way. She could always have sex with another dead-ender boyfriend.

As Dr. Reich would have pointed out, Molly had done an excellent job swallowing her memories and armoring herself against her feelings.

The Hermit wiped off his peep box and lifted the pole net to his shoulder to drain. A quarter bushel of scallops in two hours. Hardly a stellar performance. The only saving grace was that there was no one to ask how he had made out on his scalloping expedition. Which maybe, when the Hermit thought about it, wasn't a saving grace at all.

It's obvious by now that both Molly and the Hermit could have benefited greatly from some psychotherapy. But neither was ready or willing.

Which brings us to an old joke Elliott told during a speech at the American Psychiatric Association meeting last year:

How many shrinks does it take to change a lightbulb? Only one, but the lightbulb has to want to change.

12

guess who's coming to dinner

*W*hat the hell do you think you're doing? Claire said to herself.

She surveyed the Feinblat kitchen. Vegetables overflowed bowls. Trimmings spilled from cutting boards onto the black granite countertop. Pots and saucepans bubbled away on the eight-burner Wolf range under a stainless steel hood from Denmark. A rectangle of puff pastry lay partially flattened beneath a rolling pin; flour dusted the gray slate floor below it. The kitchen bore an alarming resemblance to Claire's office at Apogee.

You don't even know if he's coming.

Timers chimed. Appliances whirred. The exhaust fan hummed. Water gurgled from an Aero Retro kitchen faucet. The silken voice of Norah Jones poured out of the Bang &

Olufsen speakers, but with all the commotion, you could scarcely hear it.

It looks like you're cooking for twenty.

Claire had grown accustomed to talking to herself as she cooked in Chappaquiddick.

Claire Doheney belonged to a generation that grew up reading James Beard and watching Julia Child on PBS. She augmented her knowledge with cooking classes in Bangkok, Bologna, and Paris. One summer, she arranged a three-week apprenticeship at a Michelin-starred restaurant in Aix-en-Provence. Claire's cooking combined the practicality of someone raised in a frugal Irish Catholic household in South Boston with the precise classical culinary techniques she learned in France. Her prowess in the kitchen was legendary in Manhattan publishing circles, and during her married years, colleagues and authors would have killed for an invitation to one of her dinner parties.

Claire loved cooking for all the usual reasons and for some less obvious ones. Like most editors, Claire spent the bulk of her day hunched over manuscripts or in front of a computer screen. Cooking provided both a creative outlet and a physical release. Claire lived in a bookish world, a realm of words and ideas, and cooking gave her a way to get physical. Like most cooks, Claire cared deeply about what she ate— particularly since she had been diagnosed with cancer. When it came to ensuring the wholesomeness of the food she put in her body, there was no better way than shopping and cooking from scratch.

She also liked how cooking gave her immediate, unambiguous results. A good biography took years to write, months to edit, and many additional months of production. By the time the finished book rolled off the press, your publishing house might have a new owner, your husband might no longer be faithful, and your once lovely innocent little girl might now sport piercings, tattoos, and a mohawk. At least, when Claire cooked, she knew right away where she stood.

Had Claire bothered to plan a theme for tonight's dinner, it would have been Franco–New England. But like most instinctive cooks, Claire did her shopping first and let her menu evolve from her purchases.

At Edgartown Seafood she found a tray of freshly shucked Cape Poge Bay scallops. She had eaten bay scallops in New York, but she never tasted anything quite as buttery and sweet as the shellfish from her adopted island. According to the store's owner, bay scallops were sparse this year—hence the high prices. But what little catch came in was the best the fishmonger could remember in years. While at the fish market, Claire also picked up some alder-smoked clams and mussels.

Her next stop was Morning Glory Farm, located on West Tisbury Road on the outskirts of Edgartown. In the summer, vacationers converge on this sprawling farm stand and market to compete for limited supplies of locally grown corn, lettuce harvested that morning, and perfumed Martha's Vineyard strawberries. By this time of year, the crowds were long gone and so were the trademark bunches of colorful cut flowers in coffee cans. In fact, there was just one other customer in the store.

"Hi, Marge," Claire said to a thin woman in a Vineyard Sharks baseball cap. "I didn't see you at the survivors group last week. Is everything okay?"

Marge nodded and the two women hugged.

Marge was a fellow breast cancer survivor. Claire remembered how matter-of-factly she spoke at the first survivors meeting Claire attended. "The tumor was in my right breast," Marge said. "Luckily for me, they found and removed it early. The doctor suggested I have reconstructive surgery at the same time as the operation."

There followed a series of infections, complications, and corrective surgeries. Two years had passed, Marge joked wanly, and she still had only one and a half breasts. "My husband is a good man," she said, "but he hasn't tried to make love to me in six months."

Claire bought some locally grown leeks, Swiss chard, and an assortment of Vineyard-grown root vegetables. She sniffed some Bartlett pears from an orchard in western Massachusetts and deemed them worthy of her basket. The pomegranates, Boston lettuce, and tomatoes came from out of state—it was hard to be a complete locavore in New England during the winter. She wished Marge well and made a mental note to call the woman later that week.

Next, Claire stopped at the Farm Institute in Katama, where she had preordered a free-range chicken. The Farm Institute is a nonprofit dedicated to educating Vineyard children about organic farming. The Feinblats had taken Annabel and Nate there several times this past summer. Sales were on the honor system. Claire took her chicken out of the refrigerator and left twenty dollars in the jar next to it.

The final stop was back on Chappaquiddick, at a gray-shingled house on a dirt road near the fire station, where a hippie couple raised chickens. They sold the eggs on a first-come, first-served basis out of a refrigerator on the porch—again on the honor system. Once Claire tasted the vivid yellow yolks, she would eat no other eggs on the island.

Claire unpacked the grocery bags, and the menu began to take shape. She'd whirl the smoked clams and mussels with mascarpone cheese in the food processor to make a dip to eat by the fire. The bay scallops would be broiled with brioche bread crumbs and served on a bed of vegetables braised in vermouth. Next would come a simple salad of Boston lettuce, toasted walnuts, fresh pomegranate seeds, and crumbled Roquefort cheese.

For the main course, Claire chose a dish from her childhood:

chicken and potatoes roasted in a cast-iron pot. Of course, Mary Doheney wouldn't have used an organic bird. (*Twenty dollars for one chicken—are you crazy?* Claire smiled, imagining her mother's dismay.) And the assortment of beets, carrots, parsnips, turnips, and fingerling potatoes—also organic—was a far cry from Mary's commonplace spuds. Some weeks, Claire remembered, there were a lot more potatoes than chicken. Claire and her sisters didn't fully appreciate at the time how hard their mother struggled to make ends meet.

Everything could be prepared ahead to this stage, which would leave time for Claire to welcome her guest. Dessert—a caramelized pear tart—she would bake *à la minute* at the end of the meal. If she and the Hermit still had something to talk about, they could converse while she worked in the kitchen.

If they didn't, well, she would leave him in the dining room. She imagined he was used to being alone.

Claire beat a cup of heavy cream to soft peaks and placed it in the refrigerator. She combined sugar, eggs, and Marsala wine in a copper bowl she had purchased during her summer in Paris. She beat these ingredients into an airy mousse with an old-fashioned balloon whisk over a pan of simmering water. She let the mixture cool, beating all the while, then folded in the whipped cream. If all went well, she and the Hermit would have hot pear tart with cool creamy zabaglione.

Meanwhile, a drama of a different sort played out at a house off a footpath behind the Chappaquiddick Cemetery.

What the hell do you think you're doing? The Hermit found himself muttering to himself.

The note the woman had attached to her last gift of food lay on the table. *If you come, I will be delighted*, it read, *but I'll understand if you don't.*

The invitation presented the Hermit with a number of challenges—some logistical, some emotional, some philosophical, even some sartorial.

Among the logistical challenges was the simple matter of time: the Hermit owned no working clocks or timepieces.

Among the sartorial challenges was his wardrobe. The Hermit wore pretty much the same clothes day in and day out, year after year. "New" garments, such as they were, he scavenged from the Thrift Store in Edgartown. His peregrinations around the island took a heavy toll on his clothes, and he replaced them only when they threatened to fall apart. And even if he wished to dress for the occasion, he had no mirror in front of which to adjust his attire.

He surmised—rightly or wrongly—that the garments in which he normally tramped through the woods and waded into the waters around Chappaquiddick would look out of place at dinner.

What the hell do you think you're doing?

Among the emotional challenges was his utter isolation. The Hermit went weeks on end without speaking to another human being. When he was spoken to, he had developed a habit of responding in vague phrases and monosyllabic grunts designed to deter any further conversation. Prior to this Thanksgiving, it had been years since anyone had invited him to a social gathering and it had been more than a decade since he had sat at a table or broken bread with another human being. His voice had sounded tinny and alien when he spoke to Patrick about getting the woman to the hospital.

What would he say? What would he talk about? He had no TV or radio; he read no newspapers or magazines. He had no friends. He had no family. He would have been hard-pressed to name the governor of Massachusetts or who sat on the Edgartown board of selectmen. His social repertoire was void of all but the most superficial exchanges with bank tellers or shop clerks. If human interaction was like machinery, the Hermit's engine was out of gas, drained of lubricant, and frozen with rust.

Even if he knew what to say, there were the obstacles imposed by his antisocial outlook. For his solitude was no accident. The Hermit had made a deliberate decision to flee his fellow man. He awoke when most of the islanders were still sleeping and strode deserted paths through the woods when most people were still sipping their coffee over breakfast. The Hermit's favorite haunts weren't the crowded streets of Edgartown or Oak Bluffs, but the unpeopled marshes of Poucha Pond.

People represented one thing above all for the Hermit: danger. He did everything he could to avoid them.

What the hell do you think you're doing?

The woman seemed harmless enough. She'd returned his jacket without trying to wash it or mend it. She left him good things to eat and did not seem to expect anything in return. True, she knew where he lived, but she seemed to respect his privacy. Her dinner invitations aside, she did not go out of her way to seek him out.

He had held her in his arms and she seemed so helpless and frail.

The Hermit went outside and pumped water into a bucket. He dumped the water into an old-fashioned washbasin and washed himself as he usually did: standing and with a coarse cloth. He took a stiff-bristled brush to his calloused hands. He scrubbed them so hard, his fingers turned pink and his fingernails shone like isinglass.

He sorted through the stack of plastic milk crates that served as his dresser. He selected a flannel shirt that was almost new and put on a pair of jeans that was slightly less frayed than the rest. There was nothing to do about his wild hair, so he jammed an old fishing cap he had found washed up on Wasque Beach on his head.

If the Hermit had owned a mirror and had looked in it, he would have seen a figure that looked one part homeless, one part wharf rat, and one part Dust Bowl hobo. Perhaps it was better he didn't, for had he gazed at his reflection, he probably would have stayed home.

What the hell do you think you're doing?

Claire emerged from the shower and knotted a kerchief around her head. She put on black slacks, then changed to an Indian print skirt, and finally settled on jeans and a sweatshirt.

She started to set the table. Tablecloth? Too formal. Place mats? Too pedestrian. She opted for rectangles of batik fabric she and Sheila had purchased at the Chilmark Flea Market over the summer. She set out candlesticks and twisted the wicks of the tapers, then decided they looked too romantic. She placed votive candles in colored glasses and set them around the table. Sheila kept a big glass jar of seashells on the windowsill—a collection started when Nate and Annabel were still young enough to be entertained by gathering shells on the Chappy Point Beach. Claire scattered some shells on the table.

So how does one tell time without a clock or watch? The Hermit knew that in the winter, the Chappy ferry shuts down between 7:30 and 9 P.M. He walked down Chappaquiddick Road to the Point and waited. Before long, Patrick piloted the *On Time II* into the slip on the Edgartown side, lowered the guardrail, and went to warm up in the small cabin that served as the ferry office.

Had someone looked closely at the Hermit that night, something about the man might have seemed different. But people were so used to passing by without really seeing him, the freshly scrubbed and newly attired Hermit went unnoticed.

Claire put some Bach on the Bang & Olufsen, then changed it to Quincy Jones, then Argentinean tango music. Sheila phoned.

"I can't talk now," said Claire with a giggle. "Guess who's coming to dinner?"

She glanced at her watch: it was 7:40 P.M.

Unsociable as he was, the Hermit knew that when you went to someone's house for dinner, you shouldn't arrive empty-handed. He walked to the edge of Caleb's Pond and cut a large bunch of cattails with his Opinel. He swaddled these in some sedge grass. Then, heart beating almost audibly in his throat, he walked up North Neck Road.

You can still back out of this, he said to himself as he stood outside the Feinblat cottage. He half turned to walk away.

But the porch light went on. The screen door creaked. The woman had already seen him and was striding out to meet him.

"Hi, I'm Claire Doheney," she said, and she boldly extended her hand.

13

getting there wasn't easy

N oilly Prat," said the Hermit.

His voice croaked like a tree frog.

He took another bite of bay scallops and crinkled his brow in concentration. "Noilly Prat, saffron, sautéed leeks, tomato concassé, and a couple of tablespoons of crème fraîche."

Claire stared at him, incredulous. "How did you know?"

"Noilly Prat tastes of juniper, with overtones of coriander and grapefruit. Everyone associates vermouth with Italy, but French vermouths are more complex." The Hermit was about to mention a third country: Germany. After all, the word *vermouth* comes from the German *Wermut*, "wormwood"—one of the drink's traditional ingredients. But the woman hadn't asked.

His voice squeaked like a rusty hinge.

"No, I mean, how did you know the other ingredients I used?" Claire asked.

"When you look at a painting, you see various colors," the Hermit said. He took another bite and gestured with his fork. "When I taste this, I 'see' saffron, leeks, and cream."

His voice sounded almost normal this time, except for a high-pitched squeak at the end.

Claire had never quite thought about flavor in visual terms, but she understood what he meant. A sort of gustatory synesthesia. The metaphor was well chosen. Who was this strange man?

They were sitting at the table Claire had decorated with seashells. The flickering light from the votive candles reflected off the wineglasses and windows.

Getting there wasn't easy.

When Claire had reached to shake the Hermit's hand, he froze as though she had pulled out a pistol.

When Claire asked him his name, he paused to think how to answer for so long, she wondered if he even spoke English.

When Claire asked him when he'd moved to Chappaquiddick, he confessed he hadn't any idea of the date, the month, or the year. He didn't own a watch, he said apologetically. He reckoned time—such as he needed to—by the sun and moon and the comings and goings of the Chappy ferry.

When Claire offered him a glass of Gewürztraminer, he was so nervous, he spilled it on the afghan on the couch. Claire reached for a napkin and the Hermit lunged to help her. They clunked heads, dislodging Claire's kerchief, and once again, the Hermit saw her bald.

"I guess we're destined to meet only when I'm having a bad hair day," Claire said in an awkward attempt at humor. The Hermit sat stone-faced. Claire blushed.

When, finally, Claire ushered him to the table, he sat so far forward, you'd have thought the seat of the chair had teeth.

There followed a series of verbal false starts.

Both parties said nothing for a few minutes. Then both

simultaneously blurted out, "So . . . you like to cook?" Each beckoned for the other to speak. Neither did. Then both did. Then both were silent again.

Claire excused herself to bring the scallops to the table. Now this odd man, with his rumpled clothes, was telling her with great accuracy how he imagined she made the dish. He ate slowly, she noticed, with single-minded focus and pleasure. He seemed to not only taste but also think about each bite. He pronounced the scallops delectable and praised the cleverness of the conceit behind the dish: the Provençal rusticity of tomatoes and leeks elevated by the unexpected refinement of crème fraîche and vermouth.

"How do you know so much about food?" Claire asked.

"Where did you learn to cook?" the Hermit asked.

Claire was getting used to his answering questions by posing other questions. She told him about the apprenticeship at the restaurant in Aix-en-Provence.

"Would you mind opening this?" she asked, handing him a corkscrew and a bottle of '99 Crozes-Hermitage. She went to the kitchen to take the chicken out of the oven. She half imagined the Hermit struggling to pry out the cork with his pocket-knife.

The Hermit looked at the bottle and ran his rough hand over the label. It had been a long time since he had beheld a wine like this. He deftly removed the top of the capsule and pulled the cork in a single decisive stroke. He poured a half inch of wine into the glass, swirled it with precision, and tipped the glass to his nose. He inhaled deeply and with obvious pleasure, and for a moment Claire forgot she was sitting with a man whom most people, by appearances at least, might erroneously place among the ranks of the homeless.

Gradually, the awkward silences diminished and the hesitant questions and answers evolved into something the Hermit hadn't experienced in more than a decade.

He was having a conversation.

Claire did most of the talking, prompted by the Hermit's questions. She told him about the Feinblats, the Reich manuscript, her cancer and chemotherapy. She told him how Harrison had left her the day she got her diagnosis and now wanted to take possession of their apartment. She talked about her new bean-counting boss at Apogee and about Molly and her dead-ender boyfriends.

There was something soothing about his presence; his very reticence made him easy to talk to. He listened with an attentiveness that seemed to exclude everything else in the room.

She offered him more chicken and he eagerly took seconds.

"The French say the hardest thing to master is a perfect roast chicken," he observed. By the way he said it, Claire sensed she had measured up.

He asked her about her books. Yes, he had read the Curie book and *Mozart's Wordsmith*, Claire's biography of Lorenzo Da Ponte. (*How* does *this rough man know about the librettist of* The Marriage of Figaro *and* Così Fan Tutte? Claire wondered.) He had even read *Outside Looking In*, a novel Claire had written in the 1980s. Claire blushed again. She explained how she wrote it before realizing her true talents lay in editing other people's manuscripts—not producing her own. The Hermit—charitably, thought Claire—said the book read quite well. He didn't tell her he acquired his tattered copy from the giveaway box at the thrift shop.

You seem to like reading books about renegades and outsiders, Claire thought, but she didn't say it out loud.

By the time dessert rolled around, Claire felt comfortable enough with her guest to ask him to help in the kitchen. He washed his hands before touching food, she noticed, and reached for a steel to sharpen the knife. She gave him the pears to slice—a task he executed with surgical and staccato precision. Each slice came out the exact thickness of a poker chip, and he fanned them out with a push of his finger into a neat row of overlapping shingles. He slid the knife under the pears and transferred them to the rectangle of puff pastry. Claire sprinkled the tart with cinnamon sugar, then Armagnac, then dotted the top with butter. The oven had been preheated as hot as it would go.

"How about a glass of this while we wait?" Claire said, gesturing to a half bottle of 1976 Château d'Yquem. "It's not every day you get to toast someone who saved your life." Elliott was going to kill her.

The Hermit's eyes widened and brightened. The woman certainly knew her wine. The Sauternes shone like liquid gold and coated the sides of the wineglass like glycerin. Its scent suggested pears, flint, and bergamot, and it soothed the tongue like satin.

"Were you a chef?" Claire asked. "You move like one in the kitchen."

"Isn't there something you need to check in the oven?" the Hermit said. Claire rushed to open the oven door.

The pear tarts emerged in a cloud of cinnamon-scented smoke, the pastry puffed and golden. Another minute and they would have burned. The butter, sugar, Armagnac, and pear juices had cooked to a bubbling dark thick caramel. Claire topped the hot tarts with dollops of cold zabaglione and they ate at the kitchen counter.

Nailed it, Claire thought, smiling. The tart left the Hermit a different kind of speechless.

Claire built a fire in the raised fireplace and they finished the last of the Château d'Yquem. She made French press coffee and served it by the fire. Then she brought out the bottle of Armagnac she used in the tarts and they started to drink that.

They spoke of books and biographies, of families and food. Then after a while, they didn't speak, and that felt comfortable, too.

When Claire finally looked at her watch, she was astonished to see it was after midnight. The Hermit stood up and thanked her formally and profusely for dinner.

Claire surprised both of them by inviting him back for dinner the same time the following week. The Hermit surprised both of them by accepting. This time, his voice sounded almost normal.

It was only after he left that Claire realized she never did learn his name.

14

homesick for manhattan

The phone rang at 7:30 sharp the next morning.

Claire's head throbbed the way it did the day after chemotherapy.

"So what's he like?" asked Sheila, who had summoned every ounce of self-discipline not to call Claire earlier.

"Sheila, I have a hangover," Claire said.

"Did he change his clothes?" Sheila asked. "Cut his hair? How long did he stay?"

Discretion itself with hair like a Jewish Afro.

"He was very nice and very polite." Claire thought about the Hermit's formal diction and courtly demeanor. "Half the men in New York could take a lesson."

"And . . . ?"

"And what?" Claire said. "Let me make some coffee and call you back."

"Claire," Sheila said with a groan, but her friend stood her ground.

Claire sensed her friend had some news to share. But her pounding skull was in sore need of caffeine therapy. Besides, there was the less-than-immaculate state of the kitchen. Claire cooked with messy abandon even when stone sober, and considerable wine had flowed the previous evening. She would have been mortified for her fastidious friends to see their kitchen in its current condition. Until it was cleaned up, even talking to Sheila made Claire feel guilty.

A triple espresso and two Tylenols helped, and so did the purr of twin Bosch dishwashers.

Claire called Sheila back. The more she thought about it, the less, she realized, she had learned about her dinner guest.

"He has a strange way of answering questions with other questions," said Claire. "Maybe he was a reporter. I feel so stupid—I didn't even get his name."

"Well, speaking of journalism, I have some news," Sheila said before theatrically clearing her throat. "So, I'm thumbing through the new issue of *Publishers Weekly* and what do I see?" Here she held the magazine to the phone and crinkled a page so Claire could hear the paper. "There's a photograph of a certain Claire Doheney standing next to a certain Dr. Dante Sabati—upstaged, I might add, by a certain soap opera actress standing next to him."

Professor Sabati chaired the Classics Department at Columbia University, but his real claim to fame in Manhattan society was his recent marriage to one of the stars of *As the World Turns*.

"And I quote," said Sheila.

In this age of soft money, congressional sex scandals, and $600-an-hour lobbyists, a statesman like Marcus Tullius Cicero might seem as quaintly anachronistic as the notion of

*public service as a moral virtue. This brilliant new biogra-
phy of ancient Rome's most famous politician tells us why
Cicero's life should matter as much to us as is did to our
Founding Fathers—and to the* philosophes *of the French
Enlightenment. Old documents come alive in a new light,
thanks to the meticulous scholarship of Professor Sabati. A
venturesome work and a stellar addition to Apogee's Men of
Action biography series, edited by Claire Doheney.*

Claire thanked Sheila and smiled. "A stellar addition."
Beidermann would have had conniptions if he'd seen the time
sheets on that book.

"He's a reader, you know," Claire said.

"Cicero?" Sheila asked, puzzled.

"The Hermit," Claire said. "He seems to have read every one
of my books, even that silly novel. Talk about embarrassing."

"Nothing to be embarrassed about, honey," said Sheila.
"You managed to get it published, which is more than legions
of writers can say." They hung up.

The phone rang again a short while later. It was Beidermann calling to congratulate Claire on the *I, Cicero* review in
PW. Claire almost choked on her coffee. In the year since the
merger, Beidermann had never once complimented Claire on
her work. As Claire often told Sheila: "He's probably afraid
that if he says something nice, he'll have to give me a raise."

"By the way," Beidermann asked, trying to sound casual,
"How's the Reich book progressing?"

An alarm sounded on Claire's radar. Beidermann *never*
asked a casual question. Especially about this book. He was
furious when Claire signed it without consulting him and submitting the requisite paperwork. In his opinion, paying ten
thousand dollars to a crackpot author to write a biography of an
equally crackpot shrink amounted to fiduciary negligence.

"Couldn't be better," Claire lied. "Thanks for asking."

The moment she hung up, she phoned her assistant to find out what prompted Beidermann's sudden solicitude. The answer lay in Tuesday's *New York Times* Science section.

When Reich died in 1957, his unpublished papers went to the Countway Library of Medicine at Harvard University, where they remain to this day. His will stipulated that his archives were to be sealed for fifty years.

Due to the circumstances surrounding his death, Reich and his theories had largely been discredited. In subsequent years, some of his work—especially his body-oriented therapies— found wider acceptance. The opening of the Reich archive in the fall of 2007 generated considerable excitement in scholarly circles. The *Times* article retraced Reich's controversial career in Europe and America and named some of the scholars who were lined up to study his papers when the archives finally opened.

Once again, Claire's instincts about signing the book proved right, even though she hadn't known about the release of the Reich papers. Beidermann wanted to make sure they timed the publication of the biography to reap maximum financial return on what he initially considered a poor investment.

The truth is the book was proceeding anything but well. Claire seemed to have hit a wall. Reich called it orgone energy.

Up to this stage, Claire could follow and even agree with many of Reich's ideas—especially his belief that true mental health was impossible without a healthy sex life. Prior to her cancer and Harrison's adultery, she had enjoyed the release offered by orgasm as much as any of Reich's case studies.

But orgone energy was a lot for even the open-minded Claire to accept.

Ely had explained how, in the 1930s, Reich began studying minute particles of organic matter under a high-powered Leitz microscope. With sufficient magnification, some of these particles—*bions* the doctor called them—seemed to emit a bluish glow; others yellowish flickering. Reich called this luminous force *orgone radiation*—a neologism coined from two of his favorite subjects of study: the organism and the orgasm.

Claire warmed her hands on the coffee cup.

Faced with growing hostility to his work and the looming outbreak of the war, Reich decided to immigrate to America. His followers there had arranged a teaching post for Reich at the New School in Manhattan. He bought a house in the Forest Hills section of Queens. The doctor saw psychotherapy patients in the bedrooms upstairs and continued his orgone research in a laboratory he built in the basement.

"Is that where you first met Reich?" Claire had asked Ely.

"Yes, but not until later," the biographer said.

Reich noticed that metallic materials seemed to attract and reflect orgone energy, Ely explained, while organic materials absorbed it. To investigate the phenomenon further, the doctor built a boxlike apparatus made of alternating layers of metal and glass wool, with a lens in the front to observe what was happening inside. In time, the device became known as an orgone energy accumulator, and it would bring Reich untold sorrows.

Claire took a sip of coffee.

In the summer of 1940, Reich took a camping trip to Rangeley, Maine. Unlike in humid New York City, the air there was cool and clear, and at night, the sky sparkled with millions of stars. But according to Ely, a curious thing happened when Reich looked at the darkness *between* the stars: he saw the same bluish vapors and yellow points of light he had observed so often in the orgone energy accumulator. When he looked through a telescope, the puzzling lights appeared even brighter.

"The realization hit him like a proverbial thunderbolt," Ely said. "Orgone energy didn't just exist in the laboratory—it was a life force all around us."

Claire shook her head with incredulity. She left her desk and walked to the edge of the bluff overlooking Vineyard

Sound. The air was cold; the sky was clear; the sun seemed to dance off the waves in a million scintillating points of light. She looked at the sky, and it, too, seemed to be pulsating. But was the pulsing Reich observed truly a new source of energy, Claire wondered, or was it a phenomenon easily explained by atmospheric conditions or by some optical quirk in the eye?

She telephoned Ely. "Is it true?" she asked.

"Is what true?" said Ely.

"Is there really such a thing as orgone energy?" Claire asked.

"When I worked in the lab, I saw the bluish vapors and the yellow streamings many times," said Ely. "And when you sit in an orgone energy accumulator, you definitely feel revitalized. There's a prickling sensation and heat."

Besides, Ely added, Reich had some really smart followers, including the novelist Saul Bellow and the artist-cartoonist William Steig. His voice swelled with pride.

"If there really is such a thing as orgone energy, why didn't anyone, in the thousands of years of human history, notice it before Reich?" asked Claire.

"Most scientists think they have better things to do than to look in empty boxes and at black parts of the sky," Ely said.

"Well, do *you* believe in it, Ely?" Claire asked.

Ely was quiet for several moments. "To be honest with you," he said, "even after all these years, I still don't know for sure."

Claire sealed the edited chapter in an envelope and drove to the Chappy ferry. She boarded the boat on foot and walked up Main Street to the post office. She could have FedExed the manuscript to New York, but she always welcomed an excuse to venture into Edgartown. Besides, the next time Beidermann bellyached about Claire's Federal Express bills, she could silence him with receipts from the post office.

The Edgartown Post Office occupies the back corner of a one-story clapboard building behind the Old Whaling Church. It has but a single employee, who, for lack of a computer, still calculates postage rates with pencil and paper. You must pay cash, and during the summertime, you have to dodge swarms of tourists. Withal, it possesses considerably more charm than the large modern post office at the Triangle. Claire, like most Chappaquiddickers, preferred it.

It was there that she saw him: the weathered coat, the wild gray hair, the downward gaze and hunched shoulders. Somehow, as they talked over dinner, Claire had ceased to notice the Hermit's appearance. But now, in the light of day, he appeared to her as he must look to others. Eccentric. Derelict. Outcast.

He was fiddling with the combination lock on one of the postal boxes that lined the back wall. Post office boxes, Claire had learned, are distributed on a first-come, first-served basis. A box at the old post office means you have lived on the island for a very long time. She watched the Hermit extract a registered mail card from the box and present it to the clerk. He signed for the envelope, put it in his coat pocket, and, eyes downcast, left the post office.

What Claire did next might have surprised the Hermit. It certainly surprised her. Normally, the outgoing book editor would have called to her new acquaintance. Invited him for a cup of coffee at Espresso Love. Instead, she turned into a doorway and let him pass. It wasn't right to ignore him, to hide from him, Claire knew. But she had always done the right thing and look where it had gotten her. She fell in step a half block behind the Hermit and followed him down Main Street.

She watched as the Hermit crossed the street to avoid a band of unruly teenagers. She watched as he crossed back over after the young people had passed. She watched him stand outside Edgartown Bank, waiting for a customer at the ATM by the entryway to finish and depart. When the vestibule was clear, he went into the bank and departed a few minutes later. When Claire entered the bank, two tellers were whispering about their uncouth previous client. One looked at Claire and rolled her eyes.

The Hermit retraced his steps in his slow loping gait. He stepped into an intersection. Brakes squealed and a man in a red pickup truck shouted and honked him out of the way. The Hermit continued along Upper Main Street, past the Hob Knob inn and Atria restaurant, past Cannonball Park with its Civil War–era artillery. He continued on past the gas station and a bike rental shop—long closed for the season—and turned in at the Stop & Shop supermarket.

Claire looked around, then slipped in behind him. The Hermit avoided the meat department and bakery. He shunned the frozen food section and the aisles with the cookies, chips, and prepared foods, just as Claire would have done. To her surprise, he also passed by the produce section. He loaded up on staples, like flour, cornmeal, and cooking oil, and picked up a roll of duct tape in the housewares aisle. He paid for these items with cash from the bank envelope and loaded them into his backpack.

Claire followed him back down Main Street, left on Church Street to the thrift shop. He looked around to make sure no one was near, then rifled though a bag of clothes on the sidewalk. She watched him stop by the entrance of the Edgartown Library on Water Street, where he browsed through the giveaway book bin. He stuffed several volumes in his backpack. Then he turned down Daggett Avenue and walked toward the ferry landing.

It was an ordinary series of errands—the sort Claire had gone on dozens of times since she moved to Chappaquiddick. Yet in the hour and a half it took him to walk around town, the Hermit had not made eye contact with a single passerby that Claire could see or spoken a single word to any of the sales help. She felt like she was watching an automaton, a zombie. The Hermit managed to walk through the little world of Edgartown, Martha's Vineyard, without being the least part of it.

Or maybe not. After all, the Hermit saw the bird before Claire did. It was a seagull, and it fluttered clumsily under the roof of Memorial Wharf next to the ferry landing. The century-old covered wharf draws hordes of fishermen, who often land competition-size stripers and bluefish from its timeworn deck—despite the heavy boat traffic. Sometimes the wharf is so crowded, it's a wonder it doesn't sink into Edgartown Harbor. The downside to all this activity is the snapped fishing line, plastic six-pack collars, and other flotsam and jetsam that less ecologically minded fisherfolk leave behind.

Apparently, a seagull diving for minnows had snagged itself in a tangle of fishing line. A lure dangled from a hook in the bird's wing. The gull crashed itself again and again against the wharf's wooden columns trying to break free. But these efforts served only to ensnarl the poor creature more.

And there was the Hermit quietly approaching the creature. He moved slowly and deliberately, with unexpected grace. He gently grabbed the gull and cooed at it in a low voice. All at once, the bird stopped struggling. He removed the fishhook from its wing and, using his Opinel, cut the fishing line that entangled it. He walked to the edge of the pier and tossed the seagull into the air. It spread its wings and soared toward Chappaquiddick, its cries echoing over the water. The Hermit waited for a couple of ferries to come and go, so he could ride an empty boat home.

As Claire watched the scene, the words *noble savage* popped into her mind. The first book Claire worked on when she joined Apogee was a biography of Jean-Jacques Rousseau. The French Enlightenment writer and social critic believed that man in nature was innately good, but that society and civilization corrupted him. "Man is born free, but everywhere he is in chains," he wrote in his 1762 bestseller, *The Social Contract*. Sadly, Claire learned, Jean-Jacques's personal behavior fell short of his lofty idealism. He abandoned his five children to grow up in orphanages. Noble savage, indeed.

Claire didn't feel like going home quite yet, so she walked to Alchemy. She sat at the bar to have dinner. The man who had offered to buy her a drink a few months earlier sat a few stools down. Claire tipped her glass at him and smiled. He looked at her blankly, as though he couldn't quite place who Claire was. He turned his back and continued conversing with the woman sitting next to him. He put his hand on her thigh.

As Claire walked back to the ferry, she stopped at the Kelley House to buy a pint of hot chowder for the ferry captain on duty. She gave it to Patrick, who piloted her back to Chappaquiddick. He nodded thanks, but for once the usually friendly captain didn't have much to say. Fog rolled in over the harbor.

When Claire arrived home, there were messages from her mother and Sheila on her answering machine. She didn't feel like talking. She picked up a copy of *I, Cicero*. Normally, she would have been pleased by the *PW* review. Tonight, she wondered how many people would actually read a book about an ancient Roman statesman. True, Claire had published a number of bestsellers. But most of her books—like most books published anywhere—ended up on the remainder table.

She thought about Professor Sabati—a brilliant classicist—famous now as a soap opera star's husband. She thought about Reich and how the onetime eminent psychiatrist came to seek a mysterious energy source in empty boxes and a dark sky. She thought about Patrick driving the little ferry back and forth, forth and back, between a tourist town now dead for the season and an island all but deserted most of the year. She thought about the Hermit, how he walked through town as though sealed off in a bubble of isolation. She lit a fire and poured herself a glass of chardonnay, but that didn't seem to help either.

And for the first time since Claire had moved to Chappaquiddick, she found herself homesick for Manhattan.

15

the luckiest guy on the planet

W ho are you?" Claire said. She looked the Hermit directly in the eyes. For the first time, she noticed their color: the gray blue of open water on an overcast day.

The Hermit darted his gaze from Claire to the dessert she had placed on the table, around the room, and back to Claire. His expression suggested panic.

They sat in the Feinblat kitchen eating a meal that almost didn't happen. Claire had forgotten she invited the Hermit back for dinner a week after their first meal together. A phone call from Sheila reminded her an hour before he was due to arrive.

Did she really forget, Elliott would have wondered, or did she subconsciously wish to disinvite him after watching his lonely wanderings through Edgartown?

So Claire rushed into the kitchen and flung open the

cupboards and refrigerator to see what sort of dinner she could cobble together. "What makes a great chef?" the owner of the restaurant in Aix-en-Provence once asked during one of his nightly tirades. "Truffles? Foie gras? Raw milk cheese from a Normandy farmstead? Nonsense," the man said. "It's the ability to make something out of nothing." He explained how his culinary mentor had made bread with sawdust during World War II and carved chateaubriand from horsemeat. "Now *that* was a chef," he said.

Since then, Claire tried never to let a missing ingredient slow her down in the kitchen. But tonight's dinner would be a tall order on such short notice for a guest as discerning as the Hermit.

Claire remembered a gift from Patrick the ferryman a few weeks earlier—a frozen fillet of "striper" (as striped bass is called in these parts). She seasoned it with salt and oregano and threw it into a baking dish. She found a can of tomatillos and pureed them with a half can of chipotle chilies. She poured the resulting salsa over the ice-hard fish, grated some leftover feta cheese on top, and put the concoction in the oven.

The feta wasn't really Mexican, but it didn't make a bad stand-in for a sharp Michoacán cow's-milk cheese called *cotija*. Claire had learned about the cheese and the substitution at a weeklong cooking class she had dragged Sheila to a few years ago in Oaxaca.

She regretted she wouldn't have time to shower and change before dinner. Then again, she imagined her dinner guest hadn't spent the afternoon reading *GQ*.

Claire heated a quarter inch of olive oil in a skillet and fried a dozen cloves of sliced garlic and a couple of stale tortillas. She set the latter aside, and to the garlic she added some chicken stock from the freezer. She found a jar of pickled jalapeño pepper slices and a bunch of cilantro that didn't look too wilted. A handful of each and a squeeze of fresh lime juice, and she could turn out something approximating *sopa de lima*—Yucatán lime soup.

Claire treated herself to the cooking class in Mexico to celebrate her fiftieth birthday. Harrison had promised to take her to Cabo San Lucas, but kept finding reasons to postpone the trip. She finally went with Sheila. The course gave Claire a newfound respect for the complexity of Mexican cooking. Sheila skipped most of the classes but acquired a newfound appreciation for the mood-altering properties of tequila. The bartender at their hotel referred to them as Thelma and Louisa from Nueva York.

"Damn," Claire said half out loud. Thinking of the bartender made her realize she should make some margaritas. But she couldn't find any tequila in Elliott's liquor cabinet. So she squeezed a fresh grapefruit into a pitcher of tomato juice and stirred in the liquid from the pickled jalapeños. Sangrita is what the bartender had called the mixture. The first sip hurt, Claire remembered, but the stuff became addictive.

By the time Claire heard the timid knock on the door, she had placed a can of sweetened condensed milk in Sheila's pressure cooker. The pressure cooker had belonged to Sheila's mother, and while Sheila never used it, she didn't quite have the heart to let Annabel donate it to Goodwill. It seemed that the theme of tonight's dinner would be Mexican food from cans.

The woman looked frazzled, the Hermit thought as she opened the door. He pretended not to notice the disarray in the kitchen. He had brought her a jar of what appeared to be gray sand. Sea salt, he explained, harvested from Pocha Pond at the far end of Chappaquiddick. His voice squeaked, as it had their first dinner.

The Hermit still wore the same weathered jacket, but his flannel shirt looked of newer vintage. His hair was as wild as ever, but his face looked more engaged and alive. That's how Reich would have described it, Claire thought. *Jesus. I'm getting as touchy and feely as Ely.*

The Hermit watched as Claire poured some milk and flour into a mixing bowl, then whisked in eggs and butter. She produced two cast-iron crepe pans and set her guest to work frying crepes. She marveled at how calmly and neatly he cooked, gently swirling each pan to coat the bottom with a perfect circle of batter. When one side was cooked, he flicked the pan just so, sending the crepe sailing through the air to flip it. He always managed to land it in the pan. Had Claire been making crepes, none of them would have been round, she remarked, and half of them would have wound up on the floor.

Was it her imagination, or did the Hermit smile?

"So tell me about yourself," Claire said when finally they sat down. She crumbled the fried tortillas into the Yucatán lime soup and set a steaming bowl in front of her guest.

"Not much to tell," the Hermit mumbled between spoonfuls. The woman certainly liked hot peppers. He reached for more sangrita, then realizing that it, too, contained chili juice, asked for a glass of water. He inquired about the progress on the Reich manuscript.

Claire told him about orgone energy and Reich's purchase of a 280-acre farm in Rangeley, Maine, which he turned into a research center called Orgonon. How the handsome stone building now houses the Wilhelm Reich Museum and how visitors can rent cottages on the property. Ely had lived there in the early 1950s, Claire explained, when he served as a young research assistant for Reich. He had returned to Rangeley to be near the museum while he worked on the biography.

The conversation gave her time to open a can of coconut milk and cook up a batch of coconut rice.

"So how long have you lived on Chappaquiddick?" Claire asked.

"A while now," the Hermit said. He switched the subject to Elliott and Sheila. He wanted to know more about Elliott's books and the Mexico trip that had inspired tonight's dinner. Claire cleared the soup plates; she noticed with satisfaction that the Hermit had cleaned his bowl. She took the sizzling striper out of the oven, and the piquant aroma of *salsa verde* wafted through the kitchen.

"I don't believe you told me your name," Claire said. It escaped neither of them that her questions were becoming more pointed.

He seemed to think about it awhile; then he told her she could call him Silverman. He tried to lose himself in the striper. The salsa counterpointed the tart tomatillos with the smoky fire of the chipotles. *Damn, this woman is good.* The Hermit ate with undivided attention and unalloyed relish, artfully dodging Claire's inquiries with other questions, as he had done during their first dinner.

He nearly succeeded—until dessert. If ever there was a dessert worth speaking out for, it was this one. The pressure cooker had transformed the sweetened condensed milk into a sort of dark, thick, smoky caramel. Mexicans call it *cajeta*, but most North Americans know it by its South American name, *dulce de leche*. The Hermit had watched Claire with admiration as she spread each crepe with the *cajeta*, then piled them into a stack to make a towering cake. The caramel aroma made his taste buds ache with anticipation.

Claire cut a wedge from the cake and carefully transferred it to a plate, which she garnished with a dollop of cinnamon whipped cream. She set the plate just out of the Hermit's reach. She served herself, and as she pressed down her fork, the creamy brown caramel oozed out from between layers of crepes. A loud *uuuuuum* issued from her lips. She was laying it on as thick as the *cajeta*, and she knew it.

And now the only thing that stood between the Hermit

and this astonishing dessert was the answer to a simple question. But Claire wouldn't budge until he replied. *We can do this the easy way or the hard way*, she thought. She chided herself for enjoying the Hermit's discomfort. But one way or the other, she was determined to learn something about her reticent guest.

"Who are you?" she asked one final time. She crossed her arms and waited.

The Hermit looked longingly at the cake, then at Claire. He looked back at the dessert. "Okay," he said with a sigh. "I'm going to tell you a story.

"Once upon a time, there was a man named Silverman," the Hermit said. "Silverman considered himself the luckiest guy on the planet. School came easy. Friends came easy. His work experiences were stimulating and varied. After college, Silverman worked as a marine biologist, alternative weekly newspaper reporter, forest ranger, and a guide for a white-water rafting company in Colorado. He ran a bookstore in Connecticut and a custom cabinetry shop in Spokane."

"So where did Silverman learn to cook?" Claire asked. She decided to humor him in his third-person recital. Interesting. His voice had lost its raspy tentative quality. She moved the caramel crepe cake a little closer—but not quite close enough for the Hermit to reach it.

"After the cabinetry shop, Silverman became the manager of a sports bar," the Hermit said. "One busy Friday, the chef failed to show up for the evening service. So Silverman donned an apron and marched into the kitchen. Orders came screaming in from all sides: four buffalo shrimp; eight cheeseburgers, a bourbon steak, a nacho *grandissimo*. Curiously, in the middle of this maelstrom, Silverman did not panic. He flipped burgers, grilled steaks, glazed ribs, and plunged wire baskets full of french fries into the Fryolator. He took unexpected pleasure in plating the food and cleaning the rim of each dish with a dish towel. He even found time to adjust the seasoning in the wing sauce—a condiment he had felt for some time could use improvement.

"Silverman emerged from the kitchen at midnight, drenched with sweat, stained from head to toe with ketchup and cocktail sauce, and cut and burned from his fingertips to his elbows. He'd survived what most chefs call a baptism by fire—the first night on the line—and he was grinning as wide as the moon."

Claire smiled, too, for she remembered her first night working on the line at the restaurant in Aix-en-Provence. The chef swore at her like a legionnaire, but at the end of the evening, he uncorked a bottle of Grande Dame in her honor.

"The next day, when the chef returned to the restaurant—apologizing for a family illness that kept him in the emergency room most of the night—he found Silverman in a chef's jacket, with bandages all over his hands and forearms. The erstwhile sports bar manager said only two words: 'Teach me.'

" 'Are you serious?' asked the chef. Silverman nodded.

"The chef showed Silverman how to roll up his ankle-length apron from the waist so the hem came to the bottom of his crotch to give him the look of a culinary bad boy. Into the kitchen they marched, and Silverman quickly learned how to sharpen a knife, reduce a pile of onions or carrots to fine dice, and test the doneness of steaks by poking them with his forefinger. The chef showed him how to peel and devein shrimp with a fork and turn chicken wings into miniature drumsticks.

"The following day, Silverman bought a dozen cookbooks, which he devoured page by page in a week. He soon acquired a set of Sabatier knives and a battery of tin-lined copper pots and a solid marble rolling pin. (The chef sniffed at the latter with skepticism.) Silverman began spending less time in the front of the house and more time in the kitchen."

Claire pushed the cake to where the Hermit could reach it. He picked up a fork, but kept talking.

"A few months later, the bar's owner decided to retire. He

offered Silverman the opportunity to buy the business. Silverman's first action was to demolish the wall between the kitchen and the dining room. His lack of formal training only spurred his creativity. The innovations followed fast and furious. Poppy seed–crusted scallops with fiddlehead fern pesto. Parsnip pound cake. He was so ignorant about classical cuisine," the Hermit explained, "no ingredient combination seemed too outlandish."

Was it her imagination again, or did Claire detect another smile?

"Of course, some of the sports bar's original patrons complained about the restaurant's new direction. Some abandoned the place when the Buffalo wings became 'Bhutan wings,' marinated with yogurt and Himalayan spices. Others jumped ship when Silverman took to encapsulating a raw egg in a patty of ground sirloin. The resulting burger was flash-seared in a skillet, and when you cut into it, the equivalent of a coddled egg oozed out. Silverman called it his steak and egg burger.

"But the critics were kind to the inadvertent chef, and before long, it took weeks to get a reservation for dinner.

"Around this time, Silverman began dating a woman who had a daughter from a previous marriage. The girl's father was a jazz musician from Paris. Silverman invited mother and daughter to the restaurant and sat them at a corner table. He dispatched the maître d' to buy pillows so little Sylvie could be raised to a comfortable height. Silverman personally cooked and served their dinner, choosing simple dishes he imagined a four-year-old would appreciate, like homemade hand-pinched *farfalle* (pasta butterflies) and Rice Krispies–encrusted chicken breast. Everyone wondered who these unlikely VIPS could possibly be."

Claire shifted in her seat and forced herself to smile.

"The little girl took to Silverman like a proverbial fish to water. She'd hold his hand whenever they went out as a threesome. Far from feeling inconvenienced by having a young child tag along all the time, the chef came to consider her one of the greatest perks of dating her mother. One night, Julia Child came to the restaurant for dinner. Rebecca snapped a photo of her and Silverman with little Sylvie sitting on his shoulders."

Claire nodded for him to continue. Odd. The normally curious book editor wasn't sure she wanted to hear what came next.

"Six months later, Silverman moved in with 'the girls,' as he called them. He commandeered the kitchen, mounting his *batterie de cuisine* on the wall. He taught Sylvie how to make gingerbread cookies, rolling the dough with the marble pin. One day, Silverman brought home a cocker spaniel puppy, which Sylvie—deep in her *Wizard of Oz* phase—named Toto. And to make it an official family, Silverman married Sylvie's mother.

"The inadvertent chef settled into his new life as a restaurateur, husband, and stepfather. He was, as he often said, the luckiest guy on the planet."

The Hermit looked at Claire's dessert sadly. He set down his fork and stopped talking.

"Then what?" Claire asked.

The Hermit said nothing, as though the rest of the story were self-explanatory.

"What happened next?"

The Hermit looked down. He still hadn't touched the *torta*. He took a deep breath and continued.

"Once upon a time, there was a man who had it all. One day he came home to find his wife collapsed on the floor. She died of a cerebral hemorrhage.

"Once upon a time, there was a little girl, whom the man had come to love as a flesh-and-blood daughter. After her mother died, the little girl went to live with her biological father. The man never saw her again.

"Once upon a time, there was a chef who had a restaurant.

He lost his sense of taste and the pleasure he took in cooking. The man was a chef and then he wasn't. And as most do sooner or later, the restaurant closed.

"Once upon a time, there was a man who considered himself the luckiest guy on the planet. One day his luck ran out and he came to live on an island."

The Hermit looked up as if he were noticing Claire for the first time.

"Oh, Silverman, I'm so sorry," said Claire, and she reached out to take his hand. But already he was on his feet, the weathered coat over his shoulder.

"You have showered me with friendship and hospitality," the Hermit said, and for the first time since Claire had known him, he made eye contact with her. "I have soured your home with grief. I'm sorry, Claire, I must go."

And before she could rise to stop him, he walked out of the Feinblat cottage, leaving Claire sitting stunned at the table.

When she finally cleared the dishes, she realized that the Hermit never did taste the *cajeta* crepe cake.

16

---

not what i expected

Claire waited a day, then put a note for the Hermit and a slice of the Mexican caramel cake in the duct-taped shopping bag. She hung it on the tree at the end of the path behind the cemetery. The note went unanswered. So did a second note a few days later. The following week, the Hermit placed a letter in Claire's mailbox. He apologized for his behavior during and after what he called her electrifying Mexican dinner. He knew it must sound odd, he wrote, but he needed some time by himself.

She looked for him on the ferry and retraced his meanderings in Edgartown. Once again, the man seemed to have vanished. Sheila counseled patience—rehashing his wife's death and the loss of the little girl must have left the poor man traumatized. Surely he would resurface.

Claire buried herself in the Reich manuscript—the doctor's

tale grew ever more bizarre. Bioelectrical experiments. Cancer mice. A meeting with Albert Einstein. Ely had certainly picked a colorful character for a biography.

When the invitation appeared in the Feinblat mailbox, it took Claire a moment to place the handwriting and the sender. It was written in fountain pen on a neatly torn square of paper. The paper had been curled into a scroll and tied with fishing line to an old peanut butter jar containing a purplish substance that would prove to be Concord grape jelly. The grapes grew wild on Chappaquiddick, but in very limited quantities. They were descendants of other Concord grapes that, four hundred years earlier, had inspired Bartholomew Gosnold to name the island Martha's Vineyard.

Claire sniffed the jar's contents. She had once heard Elliott describe a wine as "foxy." She accused him of talking wine-snob nonsense, and Sheila had nodded in agreement. But there it was—a musky feral scent one could imagine emanating from a wild beast. Claire dipped her finger in the jar and licked the jam off her fingertip. It was thick and perfumed and more intensely flavorful than any other grape jelly she had ever tasted.

She pulled off the fishing line and unrolled the paper scroll. Here's what it said:

Claire,

   I apologize for my silence the last few weeks. I hope you understand. I believe it's your birthday soon. If you have no other plans, please do me the honor of coming to dinner at my house. I will meet you at the Dyke Bridge the day after tomorrow, an hour before sunset. If you come, I will be delighted, but I'll understand if you don't. There's no need to reply.

                                                                    S

Claire smiled at the awkward formality of the invitation. And at the ingenious attempt to reference time by a man who owned neither clock nor calendar. But how on earth did the Hermit know it was her birthday? Then Claire remembered a conversation they had had the night the Hermit told his sad story.

"What is your goal in life, Claire?" the Hermit asked.

In the past, she might have cited another book award or bestseller, or to see Molly happy and married.

Her wish was simpler this time: "To live to my fifty-fourth birthday."

"What's your goal in life?" she asked him in turn, and for once he didn't answer with another question.

"To not lose anything more than I already have," the Hermit said. He quickly changed the subject. Now Claire understood why.

Claire showered and knotted her kerchief around her head. A quarter inch of spiky hair now covered her scalp—thanks in part to a shampoo she had learned about at the Breast Cancer Survivors Group. It's called Nioxin and it really did seem to promote post-chemotherapy hair growth.

"You're going where?" said Sheila, horrified, during their morning phone call. "I hope you're planning to load up on Deet, Purell, and Lysol."

Sheila had a near pathological fear of bugs and germs, and she warned Claire to wear boots, socks, jeans, and a hooded sweatshirt. "I can't begin to imagine what you'll be exposed to once you get to his house. And don't even talk to me about deer ticks."

Ticks, Claire had learned, pose a threat throughout Martha's Vineyard. There are two main types and each carries a vexing disease. The dog tick, which looks like a flaxseed with legs, spreads a malaria-like malady called babesiosis. The deer tick, which is smaller than a poppy seed, has caused near epidemic levels of Lyme disease on the island; a single bite can lead to neurological and heart damage and even death.

Sheila always made sure everyone tucked their pant legs into their socks when they went hiking. She doused the children with Deet before letting them outside to play. Houseguests found reams of literature on ticks on their night tables. Sigmund, the family Labrador, remained in the housekeeper's care in New York lest he wander in the woods in Chappaquiddick and bring stray dog or deer ticks into the house.

It's a wonder how Sheila tolerates Miss Millipede. The thought made Claire smile.

She reached for her habitual jeans and sweatshirt, then changed her mind. She went back to the closet and instead pulled out a gray cashmere sweater and black suede skirt. Then, in deference to the tick-conscious Sheila, she pulled on black Bruno Magli boots. Technically, you were supposed to wear white footwear, not black, so if ticks landed on your ankles when you went tromping through the woods, they'd be easier to spot. But boots of any sort were better than shoes.

The Brunos were an extravagance Claire had treated herself to when *Mozart's Wordsmith* went into paperback. Had Mary Doheney known their price, she would have questioned her daughter's sanity. Anyway, white boots would have ruined the outfit.

She stared at herself in the mirror for a few seconds, then reached for a string of pearls. "What the hell, it's my birthday," she said to no one in particular. "I can wear whatever I want."

There was only one thing Claire dreaded—the walk through that horrid field full of junk and animal bones. Maybe that's why the Hermit asked her to meet him at the Dyke Bridge.

He was leaning against the guardrail, gazing at a silvery day moon high in the sky. When he heard Claire pull up, he walked to the car to meet her. He opened the door for Claire and ceremoniously thrust out his hand.

He's becoming more socialized, Claire thought. There was something different about the Hermit's appearance, too. He looked gentler, less ferocious. His hair looked brushed and someone had trimmed his beard—the Hermit himself, Claire surmised from the uneven scissor strokes. He wore a clean jean jacket and his work boots had new laces.

"I'm pleased you came," he told Claire. His voice sounded almost normal. He led her to the edge of the water. He had pulled the prow of his skiff up on the sand and he helped her step over the gunwales. He pushed the boat clear, waded out, and deftly climbed into the stern.

"Where are we going?" asked Claire.

"To my house," said the Hermit.

"I thought you lived near the cemetery."

" 'All roads lead to Rome,' as your friend Cicero might say," the Hermit said.

He rowed in the direction of the lighthouse to the middle of Cape Poge Bay.

"I imagine you like lobster?" he asked.

Claire nodded with enthusiasm.

He maneuvered the boat alongside a faded lobster buoy and grabbed it with a gaff pole. He hauled in the line, hand over hand, and Claire couldn't help but watch his powerful shoulder muscles flex under his shirt. He swung the lobster trap onto the stern of the boat, and with his bare hands extracted a pair of feisty two-pounders. The crustaceans waved their claws and flapped their tails angrily as he tossed them into his bucket. Claire squealed—but it was more for sport than out of any real sense of alarm.

The Hermit made no reference to their previous conversation. Claire hadn't really expected him to.

He swung the boat to shore, toward the former site of the old one-room Chappaquiddick schoolhouse. They passed a line of neat wooden piers with tidy white clapboard houses behind them. He continued rowing toward a scrappy over-grown stretch of beach, past a row of rotted pilings that once must have supported a dock. The Hermit rowed hard to push the prow of the boat on dry land so Claire could step out with-out getting her boots wet. He tied the boat to a rusted metal ring in a block of concrete.

Puzzled, Claire looked around for a house. In front of her loomed a thick wall of underbrush. The remnants of an old sloop, its hull stove in, lay half-submerged in the water. The Hermit pushed aside a fallen tree trunk, revealing a narrow path that ended at a moss-covered staircase. The first three treads from the staircase were missing, and the fourth was cracked in the center.

Sheila was right, thought Claire. *I should have worn jeans.* She wished she had put on more Deet.

"Sorry," the Hermit said. "It's a little steep here." He stood on the cracked stair and reached down to grab her hand. He did not so much help her up as lift her off her feet to a solid stair.

The stairs wound through the woods, turning to the right, then to the left, then right again, and ending at a clearing. At the back of the clearing stood a farmhouse with a peaked roof and a porch running the entire length. Its shingles had weath-ered to the gray of Claire's sweater. Flannel shirts flapped in the wind on a clothesline next to the house. A pair of chickens pecked in the yard. They came running to investigate as the Hermit and Claire approached.

Claire climbed the stairs to the porch and looked out. To her right stood a tree stump with an ax wedged in the center. Behind the stump rose a wall of neatly stacked firewood. Off in the dis-tance, a cluster of beehives. To the left grew a large garden with a man-high chicken-wire fence to keep out the deer. Claire ad-mired the neatly tended rows of winter kale and cauliflower. No wonder the Hermit avoided the produce section at the super-market.

The porch offered a sweeping unobstructed view of Cape Poge Bay, East Beach, and the wide Atlantic beyond it. Living on North Neck Road, Claire had seen some spectacular water vistas in her day, but this one left her wordless. It was all the more remarkable for being completely devoid of any other human presence.

This is not what I expected, Claire thought.

The Hermit removed his shoes and asked Claire to do the same. For a second, she was tempted to protest that she was wearing Bruno Maglis. She unzipped the chamois-soft leather and pulled off the boots. The Hermit held the door for her and ushered her inside. Claire took a deep breath, then exhaled in amazement.

Light flooded in through a wall of windows facing the bay and through a pair of skylights cut into the ceiling. The yellow pine floors had been painstakingly sanded and varnished. A massive stone fireplace dominated the back wall of the living room, and additional heat radiated from a potbelly stove with a mica window in the corner. A faded Turkmen rug lay in front of it. The room's only ornament was an old ship's bell on the mantel.

But what struck Claire most were the books. Bookshelves lined every square foot of wall, and every shelf sagged under books. Books buried an old horsehair couch; books encumbered the end tables; books covered the claw-foot dining room table and the chairs around it. Most of the volumes looked used, but a few new titles were visible. It reminded Claire of her office— only neater.

Well, I'll be damned, Claire thought. Then out loud, "How long have you lived here?"

The Hermit shook his head. "First, we eat. Then we talk."

He led Claire into a kitchen with varnished wood counters and glass-fronted bead board cabinets. Chrome handles gleamed on an enormous black wood-burning cookstove—the sort you see in grainy sepia photographs of Victorian kitchens. There was a soapstone sink and an antique pie safe and a farmhouse table with spindle-back chairs. Claire peeked in the walk-in panty. Peanut butter jars full of pickles and preserves lined the shelves.

And yet, for all its charm, there was no confusing the Hermit's home with a beach house in *Architectural Digest.* For as Claire looked closer, she notice a complete absence of the amenities of modern life. There were no lamps or light fixtures of any sort; no television, radio, or sound system. There was no telephone she could see; no cell phone charging quietly in an outlet; no blinking BlackBerry, computer, or iPad.

The kitchen had no fancy faucets or valves, but a single cast-iron spigot with a pump handle. There were food mills, hoop sieves, and mortars and pestles, but no food processor, toaster, microwave, dishwasher, or other electric appliances.

More curious still, there were none of the personal artifacts you'd expect to find in a home: no photographs in decorative frames, no newspaper clippings stuck to the refrigerator with magnets. (And now that she thought about it, Claire did not recall seeing a refrigerator.) There were no stacks of newspapers or magazines; no catalogs or mail; no CDs, DVDs, VCRs, or any of the other acronyms that supply modern lives with entertainment. There were no musical instruments; no chessboards, Scrabble sets, decks of playing cards, or other distractions you would expect to find at a beach house for a rainy day. There was no working automobile parked next to the house that Claire could remember seeing, and no signs of a washing machine or dryer.

"This is not what I expected," said Claire. She went to reach for her lipstick, then realized she hadn't seen a mirror anywhere. A panicked thought crossed her mind: *What if I have to go to the bathroom?*

As if reading her mind, the Hermit said: "There's a pump

and washstand outside and an outhouse behind the woodpile. I hope you're not disappointed, Claire. I'm afraid I live rather simply."

"Do you have electricity?" Claire felt awkward asking.

"I don't seem to need it," the Hermit said.

"What do you do for light?" Claire asked.

"Well, I normally wake at dawn and go to bed at nightfall, but I have hurricane lamps (he motioned to one) for special occasions. Don't worry about getting home tonight. There's a full moon; it will be almost as bright as daylight."

Claire went outside to freshen up. She noticed a woodstove with a large steaming pot of water and a ladle next to the wash-stand. A ladder led to a metal tank strapped to the edge of the house. The perforated head of an old watering can extended from the bottom. The Hermit's shower? She'd have to ask him.

He apologized again. "I'm not really set up for company."

"Then I'm doubly honored to be here," said Claire. "In any case, I approve of your reading material." A new copy of I, Cicero lay atop a stack of books perched on the steamer trunk that served as a coffee table.

"Something to drink?" the Hermit asked. He produced an unlabeled glass bottle stoppered with a cork and sealed with beeswax. He scraped off the latter and pried out the former and filled two glasses with an effervescent liquid.

"Root beer?" Claire asked, sniffing the glass.

"Sarsaparilla," said the Hermit. "Made from Chappaquid-dick sassafras." The Hermit explained how sassafras, which grows in abundance here, was Martha's Vineyard's first commercial export. If it weren't for sassafras, the explorer Gosnold's voyage would have ended in financial disaster. Its alleged curative properties made it a popular ingredient in nineteenth-century tonics.

Claire sipped the sparkling liquid in her glass and found it infinitely more pleasing than root beer. It was clean, aromatic, and pine-scented and less than half as sweet as a modern soft drink.

"How do you carbonate it?" Claire asked.

"The same way they make champagne," the Hermit said. "You put a small spoonful of yeast and honey in each bottle, then tightly seal it. The yeast consumes the sucrose and produces bubbles of carbon dioxide."

The Hermit set out a bowl of hazelnuts (locally gathered, he explained) that he had roasted with cinnamon sugar and sea salt. The nuts were as small as *petits pois* and as crunchy and sweet as water chestnuts.

Claire ate some and closed her eyes in rapture.

The Hermit opened a jar of what looked like tan carrots and gave Claire a long splinter of pine for a skewer.

"Pickles?" Claire asked.

"Pickled cattail shoots," said the Hermit. "You've probably seen them growing by Caleb's Pond."

Claire remembered the bouquet he had brought the first time he came for dinner.

The sun sank lower and the Hermit lit the hurricane lamps in the kitchen. Claire smelled—for the first time in her life—the mild sweet scent of whale oil. It was an aroma that few, if any, Martha's Vineyarders had smelled for the better part of a century. The Hermit added a log to the cookstove.

Claire sat on a stool at the end of the counter, where she could watch her host prepare dinner.

The Hermit chopped some ramps and venison bacon and poured a little oil into a cast-iron skillet. The scent of sizzling wild garlic filled the kitchen. While the ramps and bacon browned, he took a stale loaf of bread and grated it on an old-fashioned box grater. He added the crumbs and some crumbled dried herbs and cooked them in the bacon fat.

Next, the Hermit produced a wire basket filled with seaweed and Cape Poge Bay littlenecks.

"*Poquas*," he said. "Wampanoag for 'clams.' Time to work for your supper."

He handed Claire a bowl and an old butter knife. He showed her how to tuck a littleneck into her palm, hinge toward the base of her thumb, then gently pull the blade between the shells with her fingers. He worked with the practiced gestures of someone who had shucked bivalves a thousand times. Claire opened the clams over the bowl to catch the juices, and after a few tries, got the hang of it. The Hermit pointed to the patch of purple on the inside of one of the shells.

"Wampum," he said. "The Indians used it for jewelry and trading."

The shucked clams went on a bed of salt in a large battered metal pie pan. The Hermit had Claire spoon some crumb mixture into each clamshell and place a curl of venison bacon on top. He placed the clams in the oven just long enough to brown the topping. Soon Claire was eating the Chappaquiddick version of clams casino, washed down with a fresh bottle of sarsaparilla.

This is not what I expected, thought Claire.

The salad proved to be equally homegrown—or at least locally gathered. There were baby nasturtium shoots, wild sorrel, and borage. There were clumps of upland cress and wild asparagus stalks slender as pipe cleaners. The Hermit added some Jerusalem artichokes, which he sliced paper thin with his Opinel. He rubbed a wooden bowl with a cut ramp, adding the greens and handfuls of dried blueberries and cranberries. From a small glass vial, he drizzled the salad with home-pressed hazelnut oil. He added a few drops of maple syrup and some homemade cider vinegar, but didn't toss the salad until the last minute.

"I need to cut the lobsters in half," the Hermit warned Claire as he prepared to make the main course. "You may want to turn your head."

But Claire had seen the procedure many times at the restaurant in Aix-en-Provence. The chef had taken sadistic glee in dispatching the crustaceans at Claire's workstation. She knew that, while plunging the point of the knife through a live lobster's head and splitting it down the middle may seem barbaric, it's actually more humane than the traditional New England method of boiling the shellfish alive.

The Hermit put some clarified butter in a large roasting pan and placed it in the oven to melt. Every few months, he bought butter at the supermarket and melted it in a cast-iron pot. He carefully skimmed the foam off the top and discarded the milky liquid at the bottom. Thus clarified, the pure yellow liquid that remained would keep for several months at room temperature without spoiling. It's a staple in Indian cooking; Dr. Gupta would have called it ghee.

He seasoned the lobsters with Poucha Pond sea salt and freshly cracked black peppercorns. He placed them cut side down in the roasting pan. They hit the hot butter with a loud hiss.

When the lobster halves were browned on the cut side, he turned them over and returned the pan to the oven. After a while, he transferred the lobsters to a platter at the back of the stove to keep them warm. Meanwhile, he sliced a handful of wild onions and what looked to Claire to be fresh boletus mushrooms.

The Hermit set the roasting pan over a hot burner on the stove and added another spoonful of clarified butter. In went the onions and mushrooms, which the Hermit cooked until browned and fragrant. He added a liquid from another stoppered bottle and it flambéed in a Vesuvius-like eruption. ("Concord grape brandy," he explained.) He added a spoonful of mustard and a cup of heavy cream—the latter kept cool in the root cellar. He boiled the mixture until syrupy, seasoning it with sea salt and pepper. He poured the sauce over the lobster halves and set the platter on the table: Chappaquiddick-style lobster thermidor.

He reached in the stove's warmer drawer and pulled out a pan of johnnycakes, small Rhode Island flat cakes made with stone-ground white cap flint corn. He placed them in a basket lined with a cloth and served them with clarified butter.

He ushered Claire to a table lit by bayberry candles. She looked at him in amazement.

The French-trained culinarian and New York foodie was about to eat one of the best meals of her life, and it was made in a kitchen without electricity, gas, or hot running water.

"Thank you," said Claire, raising a glass of sarsaparilla to her host. "This is not what I expected."

17

making love to a board

How does it happen? How does the warmth of friendship spark the flame of desire and passion? How do two bodies, comfortable and companionable in clothes, come to crave the awkward intimacy of nakedness? Is it spontaneous or premeditated? Deliberate or accidental? An act of desperation or courage? Is it fueled by loneliness or abetted by one too many glasses of chardonnay—or sarsaparilla?

Does it bring pleasure or pain or a commingling of both? Profound questions all, but even Claire and the Hermit couldn't answer for certain.

Toward the end of dinner, the Hermit got up to prepare the dessert. He stood at the counter with his back to Claire. His intention was to festoon the plate with a bayberry candle. Claire rose from the table. She wasn't drunk, but she felt like it. She put her arms around the Hermit's bearlike torso and laid her head against his back. She felt the Hermit tense.

"Please," he said. But Claire did not let go. She had lost so much time already.

She felt the Hermit relax a little. They stood that way for a couple of minutes, Claire's cancer-free chest against the man's broad back. Claire breathed in his scent deeply. He smelled of old-fashioned lye soap, not deodorant. It made her Armani-scented ex-husband seem like a perfumed poodle in comparison.

"Turn around," Claire said.

The Hermit sighed. Then hesitated. Then obeyed.

"Kiss me," said Claire, and she raised her face to his. He hesitated again, then lowered his face to hers. After another second, he brushed his rough lips against hers.

It was a quick kiss, a tentative flutter of moth wings. He tried to turn his head, but Claire followed his lips with hers. They kissed longer and deeper. It seemed to Claire that she was drawing a life force from this strange self-sufficient man. The Hermit felt ambivalence, the pleasure of kissing a woman after so many years dampened by a sense of danger. He felt as if he were being drawn back into a world from which he had barely managed to escape with his life.

I wish you could say their love scene had the beauty and grace of the movies. It was, in fact, marred by the false starts and stops that had dogged their relationship from their first dinner.

The Hermit may have been a kind, gentle man, but a man he was all the same. It had been more than a decade since he had touched a woman, much less held one in his arms. Claire pressed her pelvis to his, and almost instantly, his body trembled.

The second round, they made it to the couch. Claire put her hand on the Hermit's thigh and, again, his body shook. If

Claire felt the wetness or saw him blush, she was gracious enough to pretend not to notice.

So the bad news was that the Hermit's ten-year celibacy had given him a hair trigger.

The good news was that the Hermit's ten-year celibacy had left four more rounds in the clip.

By the time they tried again, they were already on the couch. The sky had darkened and the oil lamp bathed the room in a soft glow. They were sitting facing each other. The Hermit reached for Claire's breasts. "No," she said with surprising vehemence. She intercepted his hand, moved it to her thigh, then slid it under her skirt. She was wet, he could feel, where the hair had started to grow back. Her body shuddered when he touched her.

She tugged at his fly and wrestled his jeans to the floor. She leaned over the couch and hiked up her skirt and pulled him to her from behind. This time, there were no premature fusillades and the Hermit slid deep inside her. She moaned, then he moaned, and the couch springs squeaked in unison.

They lay in a heap, their breathing returning to normal. After Harrison, the cancer, and surgery, Claire assumed her lovemaking days were over. For the first time in a long time, she felt like a woman again. *Like riding a bicycle—you never forget how.* She smiled.

As for the Hermit, he appreciated her discretion—for much as he enjoyed what had just happened, he would not have relished discussing it. (In that, Claire correctly surmised, he was like most men.) After a while, she wondered aloud what sort of dessert preparations she had interrupted. They put on their clothes—some of them, at least—and the Hermit held out a chair at the kitchen table for Claire.

Dessert was chocolate silk pie—an old recipe from his aunt Tilly. The Hermit seemed to recall that women liked chocolate, so he had made a special trip to Edgartown. The clerk at

the Soigné gourmet shop recommended a bittersweet chocolate called Scharffen Berger. The Hermit sweetened the filling
with honey from his beehives and beat the whipped cream by
hand in a battered metal bowl. The gritty crunch of the crust
came from turbinado sugar and cookie crumbs he had crushed
with an old-fashioned rolling pin.

The Hermit lit the candle and dripped hot wax on the
plate to hold it upright. All this he did with his back turned to
her; then he brought the plate to Claire and wished her a happy
birthday.

Claire was tempted to say that her wish had already been
answered. She closed her eyes instead and formulated the words
the Hermit had said to her a few weeks earlier.

May I not lose anything more than I already have.

She inhaled and blew out the candle.

After a while, they got up from the table and the Hermit
led Claire by the hand to the bedroom. It was a Spartan space,
like the rest of the house. The walls were lined with more
bookshelves and more books, but there was no dresser, mirror,
or pictures.

They sat on the edge of the bed. Something rustled like dry
leaves as they sank into the bedding. In the manner of the early
colonists, the Hermit had stuffed his mattress with the dried
fronds of bracken ferns. The toxic oils in the ferns warded off
ticks, fleas, and other insects. The normally curious Claire did
not ask about the rustling. She had bigger worries on her mind.

The Hermit had reached to unbutton Claire's sweater.
Again, she pushed his hand away.

"I should have told you earlier," Claire said miserably.
"There's nothing up there."

She remembered Dr. Gupta's words: *I will do everything in
my power to make sure you don't lose your breasts.* But once the surgical team saw the extent of the cancer, there was no prudent
choice but to perform a full double mastectomy.

Claire chose not to have reconstructive surgery for the same reason she had chosen not to wear a wig when she lost her hair during chemo.

This is what life has dealt me. This is what life gets.

The Hermit put a finger to Claire's lips. "It's all right," he said softly. "I want to make love with you, not a pair of breasts."

He stroked her short hair with his calloused fingers. "We're all wounded in some way," he said. "It's not what you have that makes you beautiful. It's what you've lost and still managed to go on living without."

"Turn out the light at least," Claire said. The Hermit snuffed the oil lamp. He sat next to her again and started to unbutton her sweater. This time she didn't stop him.

And there they were, pale ugly scars that zigzagged across her chest in the moonlight. The Hermit ran his fingers over them more gently than she would ever have thought possible for this bear of a man. He put his lips to the scars and kissed her where her breasts had been. Claire started to cry, and her tears rolled silently down her cheeks.

"It's okay," said the Hermit, and he continued to hold her and rock her. Claire cried harder now, and her whole body shook with sobs.

She cried for her illness and for the loss of her breasts and for the uncertain outcome of her treatment.

She cried for her broken marriage and for being left by her husband—good-for-nothing though he was—for a woman half her age.

She cried for Molly and their fights and for Molly's loser, slacker boyfriends.

She cried for her strange new friend, for his lost wife and child, for his solitary existence.

The Hermit held her and rocked her and kissed her, and after a while the tears and sobbing stopped. She put her arm around him, pulled his head to hers, and kissed him hard and deeply. Both parties shed their remaining clothes, and this time the Hermit lay on top of her.

Claire found her self-deprecating sense of humor. "So what's it like, making love to a board?"

"I forgot to notice," the Hermit said. Claire gave him a hug and laughed.

They panted and groaned and made all the other undignified noises two bodies do when locked in embrace. Their bodies shook in spasm at nearly the same moment. Claire started weeping again, but these tears weren't solely from sadness. The Hermit, being a man, did what most men do. He fell asleep on top of her.

After a while, the Hermit awoke and they went at it again. This time, Claire was on top and she didn't try to turn her chest away when he touched her. She wished she had breasts so the Hermit could cup them in his hands. His thrusting became more insistent, and Claire raised and lowered her pelvis to meet him.

Had Claire been her normal self-monitoring workaholic self, she would have made an insightful connection. In his book, *The Function of the Orgasm*, Wilhelm Reich described the perfect orgasm. "Tender and sensuous strivings toward one's partner," he wrote, "rhythmic frictional movements during intercourse; a slight lapse of consciousness at the acme of sexual excitation; vibrations of the total musculature during the discharge phase; and feelings of gratified fatigue following intercourse."

By the time the Hermit and Claire made love for the last time just before dawn, they had gone through every phase on Reich's checklist.

But Claire failed to make this fascinating connection. She was a woman—albeit a breastless one. She did what many women also do after lovemaking. She fell asleep in the crook of the Hermit's arm.

. But not before having one final thought about her part-ner's prodigious endurance.

Of all the men you could have sent me, Lord, thank you it was a hermit.

18

the elephants in the room

S o how did the Hermit wind up on Chappaquiddick?" Claire asked.

They were walking on a Trustees of Reservations trail between Swan Pond and Wasque Point. The Hermit pointed out the site of a failed real estate development of the 1920s called Chappaquiddick-by-the-Sea. Had the developers— moneymen from Oak Bluffs and Boston—achieved their vision, this magnificent stretch of meadow and barrier beach would now be home to 750 matchbox-size cottages. The Depression had at least one benefit, the Hermit said. The Wasque project was canceled.

There but for the grace of God, thought Claire.

It was early April and a string of warm days had melted the last traces of the previous month's snowfall. Claire had an alpaca shawl wrapped around her shoulders. Her hair had finally grown enough for her to forgo her kerchief. The Hermit wore his customary flannel, but he had replaced the rope that held up his jeans with a belt.

"My father had a sister named Tilly," the Hermit said, and it did not escape Claire's notice that he had started to refer to himself in the first person. Elliott would have pronounced this a milestone in his emotional rehabilitation.

They stopped to sit on a bench overlooking the pond and the roiling Atlantic behind it. Waves crashed on the empty beach. In a few months, the sands would blossom with brightly colored umbrellas and beach chairs.

"The Aunt Tilly of silk pie fame?" asked Claire. She thought back to the birthday dinner at the Hermit's farmhouse. And to the Hermit's prodigious performance. She blushed.

The Hermit nodded. "Aunt Tilly was the sort of relative that children find endlessly fascinating and adults would gladly forget. She was, in no particular order, a lesbian, a vegetarian, a communist, an entrepreneur, and a follower of the guru Rajneesh. In the early 1970s, Aunt Tilly went to work as a receptionist for a fledgling software company in Cambridge, Massachusetts. Instead of taking raises or bonuses, she asked to be compensated in stock options. When Lotus went public, Aunt Tilly sold her shares for millions."

Claire whistled.

"Aunt Tilly lived in unrepentant sin with her girlfriend in a converted 1890s button factory in Cambridgeport," said the Hermit. "She started buying up houses between Central and Harvard Squares. Everyone thought she was crazy—first for buying the tumbledown dwellings, then for selling them at the height of the real estate boom in 1986. The market collapsed a year later and at the bottom of the recession that followed, she purchased a farmhouse on sixteen acres on Cape Poge Bay here on Chappaquiddick."

Claire put her hand in the Hermit's hand. She still had to make the first move, but at least he squeezed her hand back.

"The farmhouse had belonged to a Chappaquiddick curmudgeon who was something of a hermit himself," the Hermit said. "He was always fighting with this neighbor or that; his lawsuits were legion and legendary. When Aunt Tilly acquired the property, she found literally hundreds of peanut butter jars scattered throughout the house. Apparently, the man had died housebound and abandoned. He preferred to subsist solely on peanut butter rather than reach out to his neighbors for help."

There's a lesson here for all recluses, Claire was tempted to say, but didn't.

They had started walking again. The mulch on the trail crunched beneath their feet.

"So what happened to Aunt Tilly?" Claire asked.

"It's a sad story," the Hermit said. "She and her girlfriend moved to Varanasi, India, to follow a guru. A month later, she stepped in front of a bus. She was killed on the spot."

"I'm sorry," Claire said.

"Much to the consternation of her siblings, Aunt Tilly left me the farmhouse and a small monthly stipend to live on," the Hermit said. "She set it up in a clever way: I have to go to town once a month to sign for and cash the checks in person. I guess she wanted to make sure I wouldn't become completely isolated."

Claire flashed on the afternoon she had followed the Hermit around Edgartown. *What on earth was she thinking?*

The trail ended in a flight of wooden steps, which took them down to a boardwalk that runs through a tidal marsh. They followed it to the beach at Wasque Point. Named for the Wampanoag words for "place of ending," Wasque marks the junction of the Atlantic Ocean and Nantucket Sound. A lone fisherman in bib waders stood in the surf, casting for bluefish. He struggled to stay upright.

"Aunt Tilly is probably turning over in her grave at the thought of what you've done to her farmhouse," Claire said.

"To the *back* of her farmhouse," the Hermit said. "Actually, I think she'd have found the abandoned house camouflage quite ingenious. But I rather doubt the grave part, seeing as she insisted on being cremated."

Claire had taken to accompanying the Hermit on his long walks around Chappaquiddick. Their weekly dinners resumed.

Neither spoke of the elephants in the room.

One day, the Hermit invited Claire to go clamming at the mouth of Caleb's Pond.

"Where are the clam rakes?" she asked when they got there, for she had often seen locals scraping the pond bottom with long-tined rakes in search of bivalves.

"Don't need them," the Hermit said.

They waded into the water. Claire shivered. The Hermit seemed oblivious of the cold. He showed Claire how to wiggle her toes back and forth in the sandy bottom, feeling for the rounded edge of a littleneck or quahog shell. She squealed when she found her first clam, and after a half hour, she was catching almost as many as the Hermit. Working as a team, it didn't take long to fill their quarter-bushel wire basket.

"So how do you know so much about foraging?" Claire asked the Hermit. She thought back to his eclectic roster of jobs.

"The first Chappaquiddickers lived off the land," the Hermit said. "I learned by trial and error."

Knowing the Hermit even the little she did, Claire suspected there was minimal error.

Caleb's Pond extends from an inlet in the Edgartown Inner Harbor to the edge of Chappaquiddick Road. The Hermit showed her the spot near the mouth of the inlet, where in 1923, some Chappaquiddick landowners proposed the construction of a bridge linking their island to Edgartown. The three-section iron bridge would have spanned more than six hundred feet of harbor, rising fifty feet over the water. The cost—a staggering $142,000 at the time—would quickly be recouped, the landowners claimed, by rising real estate taxes.

Fortunately, the selectmen shelved the project. Their lack of enthusiasm was understandable: at the time, the whole of Chappaquiddick's transportation needs were serviced by a single fourteen-foot skiff rowed by a man named Jimmy Yates.

There but for the grace of God, thought Claire.

They walked back to Claire's car, the clam basket held between them.

Another day, they hiked six miles out East Beach to the Cape Poge Lighthouse. The original lighthouse was built in 1801 by order of no less a personage than Thomas Jefferson. The job of lightkeeper fell to one Matthew Mayhew—ancestor of the sergeant who had orchestrated Claire's transfer to the hospital after the Hermit found her lying in North Neck Road. The ancestor lived with his wife and eight children in a house measuring fifteen by thirty feet.

"Can you imagine how isolated the lighthouse keeper and his poor wife must have felt?" Claire said.

"Sounds like paradise," the Hermit replied with a wink. He did that more and more these days—displayed a sense of humor. Elliott would have been pleased by his progress.

Neither spoke of the elephants in the room.

For her part, Claire resolved to introduce the Hermit to the rest of Martha's Vineyard. In the ten years he had lived there, he rarely left Chappaquiddick and had never been beyond Edgartown. Claire took him to breakfast at the Art Cliff Diner in Vineyard Haven and to dinner at State Road in West Tisbury. People stared at the Hermit sometimes. Claire learned to ignore them.

For lunch, she'd drive them to the most honky-tonk of the Vineyard's six towns, Oak Bluffs. They'd wander among the ornate doll house–size Victorian cottages painted every pastel hue of the rainbow. The cottages clustered in tight rings around the covered tabernacle of the Campground Meeting—a religious revival camp founded before the Civil War. Claire and the Hermit would lunch on lobster rolls from Giordano's—the buns buttered and toasted, the lettuce crisp, and the lobster sweet and meaty—the best, Claire had determined, on Martha's Vineyard. They'd sit on a bench near the Peter Norton House, a stately Victorian mansion overlooking the bandstand and sloping lawn of Ocean Park.

Sometimes, when the weather was warm and the sun shone, Claire would drive the Hermit "up island"—as locals refer to the western end of Martha's Vineyard. Their destination was Menemsha, a tiny fishing village that would be insufferably picturesque if it did not also possess a gritty working fishing dock. They snacked on fried clams at a fry shack called the Bite. They ordered steamed lobsters at Larsen's Fish Market and ate them dipped in melted butter on a scrappy beach overlooking the Elizabeth Islands.

The means of conveyance for these outings was as unique for the Hermit as the destination. For the first time since he had arrived on Martha's Vineyard, he saw the island from a car.

The Hermit's tolerance for crowds remained limited. More than once, Claire had to lead him out of a restaurant dining room. She'd recognize the moment when anticipation gave way to panic, and his fear of crowds became visible in his eyes. She'd take him by the hand and walk him to the ferry, and if his anxiety were especially keen, they'd wait for Patrick to give the "all clear" sign for a boat with no other passengers.

Neither spoke of the elephants in the room.

They say time heals all wounds—even irreversible surgeries like mastectomy. In time, Claire came to accept the Hermit—disheveled appearance and all—for the tender sensitive man he was.

As for the Hermit, Claire was more attentive and affectionate than his late wife—and a much better cook. The latter was not to be taken lightly. In time, the Hermit came to cherish Claire for the tender sensitive woman she was.

One day, had Claire and the Hermit looked around them, they would have seen that the elephants in the room had departed. But they didn't. They were busy. They didn't fully realize it at the time, but Claire Doheney and the Hermit of Chappaquiddick were busy falling in love.

19

the hermit's secret

Y ou bastard!" Claire says, her voice curdling in her throat with rage. "You lousy stinking bastard."

He comes out of the bedroom wearing the terry-cloth bathrobe Claire gave him as a gift the previous evening. He moves quietly, his bare feet slapping the cold wooden floor. He's thinking about breakfast. There are oysters clustered on the pilings of the broken dock where he ties up his rowboat. There are fresh eggs in the henhouse. He's planning to scramble the eggs with freshly shucked oysters and rashers of venison bacon to make a dish the old California gold miners called Hangtown fry.

Claire sits at his desk by one of the picture windows overlooking the bay. He leans over to kiss her, encircle her in his arms. He relishes the moment: once again this miraculous woman has made his life seem whole.

"You bastard!" she screams. She wheels around and slaps him as hard as she can across his face.

He steps back, uncomprehending.

"So now I know the Hermit's secret." The words spill out in a hiss.

Only now does he see the loose-leaf binder full of newspaper clippings spread open on the desk in front of her.

Claire had spent another night at the Hermit's farmhouse. She awoke at daybreak, invigorated by their lovemaking, feeling as clearheaded as the dawn. She had planned to wash the dishes they left in the soapstone sink the previous evening, set the table, make coffee—to busy herself with all the little things women do when they wake up in the home of a man who's more than a first or second date, but less than a live-in boyfriend. She scanned the bookshelves for new additions to the Hermit's library. She always scans bookshelves. Her gaze came to rest on a thick black loose-leaf binder. Funny, she hadn't noticed it before.

She knows, of course, it's wrong to look at the notebook. But she wants to learn more about this strange reticent man who holds her so lovingly in his arms.

She looks over her shoulder at the closed bedroom door, then reaches for the binder.

She'll tell him what she did later—she's sure he'll understand. He seems to understand everything.

And there it is—a *New York Times* headline as ugly as the crime it describes: CELEBRITY CHEF CHARGED IN BRUTAL SLAYING.

A photo shows the Hermit, face buried in his jacket, being ushered away from his arraignment. The yellowed clipping is dated November 15, 1996.

Adam Silver, chef-owner of the celebrated Silver Bullet restaurant near Columbus Circle, was arrested yesterday on charges of murdering his wife, documentary filmmaker Rebecca Goddard. According to a police spokeswoman, Ms. Goddard was found bludgeoned to death in the couple's West End Avenue apartment. Mr. Silver pleaded not guilty.

The late Ms. Goddard made documentary films on a wide range of topics. DA, her documentary about the day-to-day operations of the Brooklyn District Attorney's Office, inspired a popular network TV series. Bad Girls, her film about the back-alley abortions of the 1960s, received a nomination for an Oscar. Ms. Goddard is survived by a seven-year-old daughter from a previous marriage.

Mr. Silver took up professional cooking relatively late in life to become a pioneer of modern American cuisine, transforming a neighborhood sports bar into a nationally acclaimed restaurant (reviewed several times in these pages). The chef built his reputation on his unexpected flavor combinations and on his willingness to use such whimsical ingredients as root beer and cotton candy.

"Obviously, we are deeply distressed by this accusation," Silver's lawyer said. "We remind everyone, however, that in America people are innocent until proven guilty." According to the lawyer, the restaurant would close for two weeks for a previously scheduled renovation. "We are confident Mr. Silver will be exonerated," the lawyer said.

Adam Silver could not be reached for comment.

Of course Claire remembered the restaurant. How could she forget? "If you visit only one new dining establishment this year, make it the Silver Bullet," wrote the restaurant critic for *The New York Times*. BURN IN THE USA, proclaimed *New York* magazine, which hailed Adam as the "Bruce Springsteen of the American kitchen." Claire had finally gotten Harrison to take her there for their anniversary. As usual, his mind seemed elsewhere. Claire enjoyed the food, she recalled, but not the evening. Maybe that's why she failed to make the connection between the Hermit and the chef.

Subsequent articles chronicled the investigation and trial. Claire read with growing dismay as the Hermit went from being a bereaved husband to a subject of interest to a murder suspect to a convicted killer. She recognized him in the photos. Of course, his hair has turned gray and grown down past his shoulders and a thick beard now conceals his face.

Well, that explains a lot of things, Claire thinks bitterly. *Why he's hiding on this island. Why he's such a good cook. Why he doesn't seem to mind making love to a mutilated woman.*

And all the hurt and betrayal she experienced with Harrison comes rushing back. Her face burns with anger and shame.

"Open your mouth!" Claire screams at him. "Say something. Defend yourself, goddamn it."

But already she sees the Hermit's eyes have gone dead, his face blank, his shoulders hunched over. The Hermit says nothing. He doesn't even try to explain.

Claire runs into the bedroom and gathers up her clothes. She leaves without saying another word. She stumbles through the junkyard to the path behind the cemetery, boots tripping over deer skulls. She runs down the long dirt lane to Chappaquiddick Road. She flags down a passing pickup truck to take her to her car at the Dyke Bridge. The driver, astonished to find a woman hitchhiking so early in the morning, turns to make conversation. Claire gives him a look of such rage, he says not a word until they reach the bridge.

Her car is right where she left it, next to the bridge where another woman died at the hands of a faithless man. *What were the passenger's last thoughts as the senator's car filled with water?*

Claire wonders. She jumps in the vehicle, fumbles with the key, and roars down North Neck Road.

The Hermit gathers the newspaper clippings and puts them back in the binder. He washes and dries the dishes. He smooths the bed linens and fern-stuffed mattress back the way they were the previous morning. He puts on his patched jeans and a flannel shirt with holes in the elbows. He grabs his formerly orange, duct-taped jacket and lopes forlornly into the dawn.

20

my great taste in men

Claire arrived home lucky not to have run over any deer. She slammed the door and built a roaring blaze in the fireplace. She stripped off her clothes and threw them in the fire. She turned on the shower as hot as she could bear. She let the water pound her for thirty minutes, her tears mingling with the soap. She scoured her chest and thighs with a scrub brush. The zigzag scars where her breasts had been stood out pale against her red skin.

She threw on jeans and a sweatshirt and went to the kitchen. She grabbed a small wooden carving of a pilot whale that lay on the breakfast table and took it out to the woodpile. She swung the ax and reduced the object to a pile of splinters. With each blow, she tried to imagine splitting the Hermit's skull.

You bastard. You bastard. You bastard.

The ax landed with dull thuds.

Nice choice, Claire. You sure know how to pick 'em. First, a philandering college professor who beds students as young as Molly.

"But even Harrison looks good compared with a wife murderer." Claire said it half out loud, but for once her self-deprecating sense of humor failed her.

Well, now Claire understood just why the Hermit had been so reluctant to meet Sheila. She flashed back to a conversation that took place a week earlier at the Feinblat breakfast table.

"She won't bite," Claire had said. She forced a smile and looked the Hermit in the eyes. Or tried to.

The latter kept his gaze on a block of beetlebung wood he whittled with his Opinel knife. Thin shavings of the hard wood—native to Martha's Vineyard and once used to plug barrels—grew in a pile on the newspapers Claire had spread on the table. The contours of a pilot whale—the blunt bottle bottom head, the graceful crescent-shaped tail—began to emerge from the wood.

If the Hermit was aware there was another person in the room, he didn't show it.

What did this woman want from him? Each time he became comfortable with Claire, she tried escalating their level of intimacy. Car rides. Candlelit restaurants. Hand-holding on the beach. Hadn't he emerged from his shell enough?

He pressed the knife to the wood more forcefully. But all these activities paled in comparison to Claire's current request: lunch with her girlfriend Sheila.

"She won't bite," Claire said again.

Had the Hermit consulted his buddies, one of them would have explained Claire's insistant entreaty. *This is what women do. When they meet a new guy and they think it's serious, they need validation from a girlfriend.*

The Hermit, however, had no buddies—male or otherwise—so he didn't fully grasp the significance of Claire's request.

"You don't know anything about women," Claire said in

frustration, and for the first time that afternoon, she and the Hermit agreed about something.

She stood in front of the Hermit and crossed her arms, blocking the light from the window. "Sheila Feinblat has been my best friend since college," Claire said. "She graciously lent me this house. She's the reason I'm here on Chappaquiddick. And, indirectly at least, the reason I met you. She'd like to meet you and I don't think it's too much to ask for you to have lunch with us."

Okay, so she stretched the truth a little. Sheila had never expressly asked to meet the Hermit. On the contrary, like any good friend would, she worried about a relationship between a cultured Manhattan book editor and a vagabond recluse. But she kept her fears to herself. If the Hermit made Claire happy, well, he made Sheila happy, too.

"Damn," the Hermit said. The Opinel slipped, taking off a tail detail the Hermit had spent the last fifteen minutes carving. Claire looked at him, shocked. She had never heard him curse.

Blood reddened the beetlebung whale carving and dripped onto the newspaper. The wayward knife had also sliced the Hermit's thumb. "Damn," he said again, and put the wounded appendage in his mouth.

"Let me see it," Claire said. Blood ran from a deep gash in the side of his thumb. She rushed to the utility room and rummaged to find a first aid kit.

She returned to find the Hermit uncorking a bottle of Elliott's vodka. He had taken a darning needle and fishing line from his coat pocket and sterilized them with the alcohol. He poured more vodka over the wound, then stitched it up with no more ceremony than if he were mending one of his flannel shirts.

Claire turned as pale as one of her manuscript pages and sat down so as not to faint.

"For Chrissake, if you really didn't want to meet Sheila," she said, "all you had to do was say so."

They didn't talk much the rest of the day, and the Hermit left after dinner.

Claire let the subject drop. Neither mentioned lunch with Sheila again when Claire returned to the Hermit's house the following weekend. Well, now the Hermit's reluctance made sense.

Claire still felt dirty, so she took another shower. She stormed into her office and tried to lose herself in the Reich manuscript. Like many overachievers, Claire dealt with emotional stress by burying herself in her work.

The doctor, too, turned out to be a criminal and a fraud—unmasked by the Food and Drug Administration and in United States Federal Court.

Is no one what he seems? Claire sighed.

Reich believed that orgone energy had curative powers. He set out to see if it could treat mice he had injected with cancer. He built a special accumulator and placed the cancer mice inside. According to Ely, the results were startling: The untreated mice died in four weeks; the mice in the orgone box were still alive after two and a half months.

In December 1940, Reich built an accumulator large enough to hold a human. It looked like a phone booth made from sheet metal and Celotex insulation. He used the device to treat patients with terminal cancer. He promised no cure and he accepted no payment: he took pains to spell out the experimental nature of the accumulator.

The words on Ely's neatly typewritten pages seemed to swim in Claire's tear-filled eyes.

Death did occur in all fifteen cases Reich treated between 1941 and 1943—as eventually it does for all of us. Three patients died in the interval predicted by their physicians. Six patients lived five to twelve months longer than expected. Six patients were still alive three years later when the study ended. In several cases, the tumors shrank in size. More significant, all the patients reported dramatic relief from their pain. It indeed seemed that orgone energy, Ely wrote, could be harnessed to fight cancer.

Wonderful, thought Claire. *A cancer quack. Why waste time with surgery and chemotherapy when you could sit in an orgone energy box?*

The phone rang, shattering the morning silence.

"Soooooooo," Sheila said slyly. "Someone didn't answer her phone last night."

Claire could imagine the knowing grin on Sheila's face and cut her off. "A murderer. A homicidal maniac!" she screamed into the phone.

Sheila wondered if Claire had relapsed into chemotherapy-induced dementia. "Whoa," she said. "Calm down and tell me what happened."

"Do you remember that restaurant scandal back in the mid-1990s? The place near Columbus Circle whose chef murdered his wife?"

"The Silver Bullet?" Of course Sheila remembered. The trial mesmerized Manhattan foodies. For weeks they spoke of little else.

"Well, you know my great taste in men," Claire said. "The chef turns out to be the Hermit of Chappaquiddick, and last night I slept with him."

"Ouch," said Sheila. For once the loquacious children's book editor didn't know what to say.

Claire asked her friend what she should do. Notify the authorities? Or kill him?

"What makes you so certain he's guilty?" Sheila asked.

Harrison's face flashed before her. "Well, for starters," Claire said, "he's male."

Claire spent the rest of the day alternately plowing through

Ely's manuscript and crying. The doctor's saga grew stranger with each page.

Reich had a neighbor in Maine named Herman Templeton. In 1940, the dyed-in-the-wool Yankee contracted a terminal case of cancer. The doctor persuaded his skeptical friend—now near death—to construct an orgone energy accumulator. After a few months of treatment, Herman's cancer went into remission. Templeton became enough of a believer in orgone energy to go into business building accumulators for Reich to distribute to his patients.

For a business it had become, Ely explained. By 1947, orgone energy therapy had captured the interest of a new generation of American physicians and psychotherapists. Accumulator rentals provided a significant source of revenue for the newly founded Wilhelm Reich Institute.

Unfortunately for Reich, his accumulators also caught the attention of the Food and Drug Administration. In 1947, the FDA sent an inspector to Orgonon to investigate. The fifty-year-old Reich met the straitlaced inspector dressed in his customary dungarees and work shirt. "He looked anything but respectable," the man wrote in his report. Local rumors about the doctor's eccentricities and wild orgies at Orgonon among Reich's research assistants didn't help the doctor's case either.

The latter were not entirely unfounded, Ely confided with a grin.

The FDA investigation culminated in an injunction against the doctor and his Wilhelm Reich Foundation. It denied the existence of orgone energy and declared the accumulator worthless. By transporting it across state lines, Reich had broken federal laws and trafficked in human misery.

Claire thought back to the Hermit's sad story. He hadn't actually lied to her. He just didn't tell the whole truth.

It was at this juncture that Reich made what in Ely's mind

was a fatal decision. He refused to appear in federal court to defend himself. Instead, he submitted a written Response to the Court. "Matters of science should be decided by scientists, not by lawyers or judges," Reich wrote.

Even the Hermit's pseudonym rang true. His family name was Silver. And he certainly was a man. Claire flushed at the thought of their lovemaking.

Had Reich chosen to defend himself in person, Ely believed, the government's case would have collapsed. After all, the FDA had interviewed more than a hundred orgone energy accumulator users. Not a single dissatisfied customer could be found.

In the wake of the doctor's "no-show" in court, the FDA lawyers had a field day. The injunction ordered the destruction of all accumulators—even those being used by satisfied patients. More ominously, it also ordered the destruction of all in-stock copies of Reich's publications, like the *Orgone Energy Bulletin*. All hardcover copies of Reich's books were ordered withheld from distribution—until such time as Reich deleted all references to orgone energy in them.

It was one of the most drastic instances of censorship in American history, yet virtually no one outside of Reich's circle uttered a word of protest.

Ely's anger roared off the page. *Damn good writing*, thought Claire. For the first time that day, she allowed herself a smile.

The phone rang again. This time it was Elliott. He sympathized with Claire on the awkward turn of events. Elliott seemed to recall some ambiguities about the Hermit's case. He promised to do some research and get back to her. "On the bright side, letting some romance back into your life is a bold step forward and a powerful part of the healing process," Elliott said.

"When I need a psychiatrist, I'll call you," Claire said. She slammed down the phone.

As for Reich, a year later he found himself back in court charged with contempt of the FDA injunction. The doctor had embarked on a research trip in Arizona. In his absence, a colleague arranged for the transfer of a truck full of accumulators and Reich literature from Orgonon to New York City. The FDA intercepted the shipment.

By this time, the pressures of the FDA persecutions and the various trials had begun to impair Reich's reason. His defense included incoherent ramblings about a grave planetary emergency and orgone energy–powered spaceships; about shadowy enemies called HIGS—Hoodlums in Government—and secret friends in the United States Air Force.

Here Ely's sadness was palpable. Whether right or wrong in his theories, Ely argued, Reich had devoted virtually his entire life and fortune not to enriching himself, but to bettering the condition of mankind.

Two weeks after the ill-fated discovery of the Hermit's notebook, Claire left the Feinblat house for her daily walk. But when she reached Chappaquiddick Road, she turned left toward the Chappy Store.

What are you doing, Claire? she asked herself.

She passed the store and turned onto the dirt lane leading to the cemetery. A line from Ely's manuscript haunted her: "Suspend judgment until you really know all the facts."

Are you insane? Turn back. Claire walked through the gravestones, found the narrow trail, and trod through the boneyard to the Hermit's back door.

She knocked and waited a long time. When the Hermit finally answered the door, he looked like the man she first saw walking on Chappaquiddick Road during a thunderstorm. Shoulders hunched. Hair uncombed. Beard ragged. Frayed flannel shirt and patched jeans belted with a length of boat rope.

Claire looked the Hermit hard in the eyes. "Did you really murder that woman?" she asked.

21

the ladder of law

So once again, Claire found herself on the old horsehair couch in the Hermit's living room. The blazing logs in the fireplace had long since burned down to embers. Night had fallen without her noticing, and the glass of sarsaparilla the Hermit had poured stood untouched on the coffee table. She sat in a Chappaquiddick farmhouse, but her mind was still in a Manhattan courtroom, trying to make sense of the Hermit's story.

The Hermit had spoken in a faraway voice, as though the events he recounted had occurred not only long ago, but also to someone else, a distant acquaintance he barely knew.

The trial had begun in New York Criminal Court eleven months after the slaying. The press had a field day. MURDER MOST FOWL screamed a 60-point headline on the front page of *The Daily News*. Even the normally staid *Times* referred to the trial and its impact on the Manhattan food scene as A MASSIVE CASE OF HEARTBURN.

Claire vaguely remembered the headlines.

Adam, the Hermit explained, sat next to his attorney, Mandy Greene. The woman came recommended by one of the restaurant's regular customers, a high-powered intellectual property lawyer. "Don't be deceived by her appearance," the man warned. "She has the mind of Machiavelli and the appetite of a shark."

Adam had his doubts. His attorney scarcely looked old enough to have graduated from law school. She rode her bicycle to the Manhattan courthouse every day and carried the legal documents in her backpack. Mandy Greene did not wear makeup. She did not eat meat. She scrupulously avoided leather or any product that required the death of an animal. The Machiavellian shark may have made the *Harvard Law Review*, but she wouldn't have looked out of place distributing PETA flyers on a West Village street corner.

Adam wore a black Hugo Boss suit—a welcome change from the orange Rikers Island jumpsuit in which he had appeared at the various pretrial proceedings. After his arrest, he was denied bail. The investigators had found his passport with a couple of changes of clothes in an overnighter bag in his office at the restaurant. Adam explained that he had been scheduled to appear as guest chef at a culinary event in Montreal the week following the murder. "Flight risk," said the prosecutor. The judge concurred.

"All rise," said the bailiff as the judge walked in. The Honorable Penelope Hamburg strode to the bench in her black robe, her platinum hair pulled back in a bun. She took her seat and pounded her gavel.

"Case number CR-000420-G, in the matter of *The People versus Adam Sil*ver in a case of first degree murder," announced the bailiff.

Judge Hamburg turned to Greene. "How does your client plead to these charges?"

Claire felt the full weight of the accusation press down on her.

"Not guilty," Greene said, her voice barely audible in the packed courtroom.

The prosecutor was a bull terrier of a man named Angelo Manzo. He wore Brooks Brothers suits and spoke with a heavy Brooklyn accent. He had put in his time at the DA's office for five years and this case was his payoff. A high-profile win, with the conviction of a celebrity, would springboard him to his real goal: a career in politics.

"Ladies and gentlemen of the jury," he said with grave flourish, launching into his opening argument. "This case is about the cold-blooded murder of one of America's most gifted filmmakers. A homicide doubly horrifying because the victim was the murderer's wife. In taking Rebecca Goddard's life, this man [here the prosecutor gestured contemptuously to Adam] robbed a little girl of her mother, deprived the community of an artist, and took an innocent young woman's life."

Mandy Greene's wardrobe and courtroom conduct inspired considerable commentary. The defense attorney favored short skirts or long Indian-style tunics over trousers. She took notes by hand in minuscule script on reams of recycled paper. She sat cross-legged in her chair and had a habit of listening to the proceedings with her eyes closed—a posture that made her look like she was meditating.

The prosecutor intended to take the jurors step-by-step through the brutal slaying. Testimony would be heard not only from expert medical and forensic witnesses, but even from one of the defendant's close friends. "True, the accused is a public figure," Manzo said, his voice booming. "But here in this courtroom, in this fair state of New York, I intend to show that even for a celebrity, the ladder of law has no top and no bottom."

"He cribbed the line from a Bob Dylan song," Adam whispered to Greene. He wondered if his attorney was old enough to know who Bob Dylan was.

"The Lonesome Death of Hattie Carroll." Claire knew the song.

Despite the flamboyance of the opening statement, the trial unfolded as most do—a tedious procession of courtroom procedure, expert witness testimony, and a slow aggregation of facts.

The jury heard a recording of the call placed to a 911 operator on Tuesday, November 12, 1996, at 11:34 P.M.

"My wife—she's been hurt," the caller said. "Please send an ambulance." The tape was punctuated with beeps. The voice was Adam Silver's.

"Is she conscious or unconscious?" the operator asked. "Do you see any signs of assault?"

"I think she's still breathing, but I can't wake her." The voice sounded strangely dispassionate. It gave the address of a West End Avenue apartment.

The jury heard the report from an emergency medical technician, who arrived on the scene at 11:49 P.M. "The patient lay facedown on the kitchen floor," the technician said. "She had massive lacerations on the back of her head and a significant loss of blood. We collared and long-boarded her and started an IV."

"Collared and long-boarded?" asked Manzo.

"Immobilized her head and neck in a cervical collar and strapped her to a carry board—we do this in any case involving severe head injury."

"Where was the defendant during all this?" asked Manzo.

"He sat on the kitchen floor next to her," the EMT said.

Manzo gave the jury a significant look, but asked no further questions.

The next witness was one of the responding officers who arrived on the scene as the EMTs were transferring the victim to a gurney. There was blood everywhere, including on the defendant's hands, sleeves, and soles of his shoes, the officer testified. "The man wanted to accompany his wife in the ambulance to the hospital. I sent my partner to take him in a patrol car."

"Why was that?" Manzo asked.

The officer looked at Adam. "We didn't know this was a murder case yet, but we couldn't rule out domestic violence."

The court heard next from a young woman with short-cropped hair, the physician on duty that night in the emergency room at St. Luke's Hospital on West Fifty-ninth Street.

"We admitted Ms. Goddard at 12:09 A.M.," the doctor said. "She had sustained a severe head injury with intracranial hemorrhaging and cerebral edema. She was obtunded—profoundly unconscious—and did not respond to voice or painful stimulus. I intubated her to protect her airway."

"Did you stitch up her wound?" Manzo asked.

The doctor shook her head and said no.

"Why not?" asked Manzo.

"She scored a three on the Glascow Coma Scale, and he bedside electrocephalogram showed only minimal cerebral a tivity."

"Which means?"

"Essentially, she was brain-dead."

"What happened next?"

"Ms. Goddard's condition deteriorated. At 3:05 A.M. v her on a ventilator. At 5:43 A.M. we pronounced her dea

The prosecution called New York City Medical Ex Dr. Robert Pilz, to explain cause of death. Manzo est

his credentials—Tufts School of Medicine, residency in pathology at Johns Hopkins, and eighteen years in the New York City Medical Examiners Office.

"Did you perform an autopsy?" asked Manzo.

Dr. Pilz nodded, using a pull chart to explain his findings. Ms. Goddard was a thirty-nine-year-old woman, otherwise healthy except for the injuries to her head. Those injuries included a broken nose (likely sustained when she fell) and multiple crescent-shaped lacerations on the left occipital scalp, with corresponding skull fractures and severe subdural bruising.

"Multiple fractures?" asked Manzo, feigning surprise. "Good Lord, how many times was the poor woman struck?"

"A minimum of six to eight times," the medical examiner said.

Claire could not help but shudder.

"How did she die, Doctor?" Manzo asked.

"The brain sits in a sort of rigid bony box, the skull," explained Dr. Pilz. "An injury like this causes severe swelling; the brain has nowhere to go but through a hole in the base of the skull called the foramen magnum. The process is called herniation and it crushes the part of the brain that controls breathing, blood pressure, and the heart rate. The actual cause of death was ventricular fibrillation."

"Could you explain what happened in layman's terms?" Manzo asked.

"Someone bashed her brains so hard, her heart stopped."

"Did you reach a conclusion as to the manner of death?" Manzo asked.

"I did," Dr. Pilz said. "Homicide."

According to the medical examiner, the time of injury was between 3 and 6 P.M. The attacker struck from behind. Rebecca never knew what hit her.

"And what could have caused such a devastating wound to cost this talented woman, this young mother her life?"

"A blunt object."

"Like this?" asked the prosecutor innocently, picking up a long, slender grayish white cylinder. The medical examiner nodded. The crescent-shaped wounds were consistent with being struck by the end of such an object.

Judge Hamburg called a recess.

Claire let out a sigh.

When the trial reconvened, the homicide detective in charge of the case took the stand. The woman's husband and the EMTs had disturbed the crime scene, the detective said. Nonetheless, an exhaustive search of the kitchen, the rest of apartment, and the basement of the building gave the investigators a clear picture of what had happened.

The woman had been drinking wine—a 2007 Marlborough Sauvignon Blanc—the detective added, glancing at a small notebook. "We found the half-empty bottle on the counter and a shattered wineglass on the floor."

At some point, someone else entered the apartment—either an acquaintance of the decedent or someone with a key.

"What makes you think that?" the prosecutor asked, looking at Adam.

"The lock and door were intact," the detective said.

It turned out that whoever entered the apartment was on familiar enough terms with Ms. Goddard to have been offered or helped himself to a glass of wine.

"I thought you mentioned a single wineglass on the floor," said the prosecutor.

"There was a second wineglass," the detective said. "We found it in the Dumpster at the bottom of the building's trash chute."

"Did it have any fingerprints on it?" asked the prosecutor.

The detective nodded and gestured to Adam. "The defendant's."

"Did you find anything else in the Dumpster?"

The detective pointed to the slender white cylinder. "The murder weapon."

Prosecutor Manzo picked up the object with both hands and walked it to the jury. "What is this?" he asked.

"It's a marble rolling pin," the detective answered. The gray white cylinder had a rust-colored spot at one end. "It's smooth, heavy, and cold," the detective observed. "Apparently, when it comes to rolling out pastry, nothing beats it."

"We'll ignore the pun," Manzo said. A couple of the jury members winced.

"How do you know it was used to slay Ms. Goddard?" asked Manzo.

The detective pointed to the rust-colored spot. "The victim's blood and a few strands of her hair are on it."

"Were there any fingerprints?" asked Manzo.

The detective looked at the crime lab report and nodded. "The defendant's."

"Gee, this doesn't look like what my mother used to roll pie dough with when I was growing up," Manzo said. He made a show of straining to lift the marble rolling pin. "Who would use such a large, heavy, and I imagine expensive rolling pin?"

"A professional chef, I guess," the detective said.

"I guess you're right," said Manzo, producing a copy of a receipt from Williams-Sonoma, dated a few days after Adam's culinary epiphany at the sports bar. He walked back and forth, lost in thought, as though he were trying to figure out a puzzle.

"I don't know how to say this delicately, but if you hit someone with such a heavy object hard enough to fracture her skull, it must make quite a mess." A woman in the jury box winced. He picked up a bloodstained chef's coat. "What can you tell us about this?"

"We also found it in the Dumpster. The blood on it belonged to the victim. The size and brand of the jacket were the same as the coats the suspect normally wore at the restaurant."

Manzo called another witness, a neighbor who swore she heard a heated argument coming from the West End Avenue apartment the day of the murder.

The following week, Prosecutor Manzo called his final witness: Adam's erstwhile sous chef and friend, Tim Dobbins. The young man wore an ill-fitting sports coat and tie—clearly not his own. Freshly shined black clogs extended from his houndstooth chef pants. Yes, he was working at the restaurant the afternoon and night of the murder. Yes, Chef left after the lunch service at 3 P.M. and didn't return until after 6 P.M. No, there was nothing unusual about this. Most chefs took a break between lunch and dinner to shop for supplies, go for a walk, or take a nap.

"What was Adam's mental state the week leading up to the murder?" asked Manzo. "Did he seem odd or in any way stressed?"

Dobbins delivered a nervous monologue about the stresses of running a three-star restaurant in Manhattan. He challenged the prosecutor to find a single chef in New York who *didn't* seem odd or stressed. But even in the pressure-cooker environment of a professional kitchen, Adam remained uncommonly calm and respectful. "He's the most even-keeled chef any of us have ever worked for," Dobbins said.

The prosecutor tried another approach. Cooking on the line at a restaurant like the Silver Bullet must be a very intense experience. Comradely. Even intimate. Dobbins nodded. Chefs must talk about personal stuff over a beer after work.

Had Dobbins met Rebecca? the prosecutor wondered aloud.

"Of course," Dobbins said.

"Were the chef and his wife happily married?" asked Manzo.

Dobbins looked down at his clogs and said nothing.

"Mr. Dobbins," Manzo said. Tim remained silent. "Mr. Dobbins." Manzo raised his voice. "I remind you, you're under oath in a court of law. I ask you again, did Adam ever suggest that he had marital problems?"

Dobbins sighed. He looked at Adam. The latter nodded. "One evening after work, Chef asked if he could spend the night at my apartment. He told me that Rebecca had asked him to move out." The sous chef seemed to crumple in the witness chair. He left the witness stand stoop shouldered, and didn't quite dare look at Adam.

Contrary to Adam's initial impression, Ms. Greene put on a highly effective defense. She spoke in a calm voice so low, the judge and jury members had to lean over to hear her. She cross-examined witnesses in such a deferential manner, they were scarcely aware they were being discredited. The crime lab technician was shown to have lied about her immigration status. The medical examiner turned out to have graduated at the bottom of his class at Syracuse. The detective from New York City Homicide stood accused of domestic violence and currently had a restraining order on him from his ex-wife.

Greene's meticulous research raised all sorts of troubling questions about the police handling of the evidence. Didn't Ms. Goddard have an editing studio in the West End Avenue apartment? Wasn't there a constant steam of editors, researchers, interns, and underwriters? The neighbor certainly thought so and she admitted to complaining to the co-op association about the foot traffic. Greene asked the investigators for a complete list of all persons who had been to the apartment in the past six months. She expressed her astonishment— and dismay—when the police were unable to produce a corresponding list of alibis for each of those persons on the day of the murder.

With regards to the second wineglass, she asked if there had been wine in it or if saliva had been found on the rim. The lab technician replied no to both questions. "So someone could have taken a clean glass from the cupboard and thrown it down the trash shoot?" Greene asked. "Of course Adam's fingerprints would be on the glass in the Dumpster—he lived in the apartment." The technician was forced to agree.

The rolling pin posed similar problems, for while there was no denying the presence of Adam's fingerprints on the marble, naturally he would have used the pin any number of times to cook for his family. "No, what puzzles me is this," she said, asking for a blowup of the fingerprints. She pointed to a smudge at the end of the pin. "What would have caused this?"

"Maybe a glove," the technician said.

"It doesn't make sense," Greene said, as if musing to herself. "Why would someone allow his fingerprints to be all over an object, then wear gloves the last time he used it?"

The technician had no explanation.

The bloodstained chef's coat also troubled the young attorney. Ms. Greene confessed to being addicted to crime scene TV shows, and here she looked knowingly at the jury. On television, at least, strike wounds produced a fine spattering of blood, not the large stains on the coat. "If I didn't know better," Mandy Greene said, "I'd say this jacket looks like it was used as a floor rag." The crime scene investigator admitted that the stains were more typical of mopping up blood than spatter marks. Yes, they could easily have been applied after the woman was beaten.

"So you can't say with certainty that the perpetrator— whoever he or she was—wore this jacket when Ms. Goddard was killed?"

The investigator said he could not.

With regards to Adam's whereabouts, Greene could, of course, produce a courtroom full of chefs who took the afternoon off between the lunch and dinner service. As everyone had heard, Adam was a patient employer who handled the pressures of working in a hot kitchen with remarkable equanimity. Perhaps he had marital problems (most people do at some point), but by all accounts he was a good husband and devoted stepfather. There was simply no evidence to suggest that Adam Silver was capable of murder.

When it came time for closing arguments, Angelo Manzo strutted like a peacock. "We have a victim," he told the jury. "We have a murder weapon. We have a motive. We have fingerprints and other scientific evidence and it all points to this man here." He flung his arm toward Adam. "All we need, ladies and gentlemen of the jury, is a conviction for first degree murder."

"Closing arguments, Ms. Greene?" asked Judge Hamburg. "Ms. Greene?"

Adam's attorney looked lost in thought. Today she wore a dashiki over saffron-colored leg wraps. The fabrics were natural, of course, woven by a third-world women's collaborative.

"Ladies and gentlemen of the jury, we've just heard some terrible accusations," Ms. Greene said. She paused for a moment. "What I'm beginning to wonder is whether we have the right man on trial."

Ms. Greene turned to face prosecutor Manzo. "What is it the Bible says? 'Let he who is without sin cast the first stone'?"

Prosecutor Manzo drummed his fingers.

"Your Honor," she said, turning to Judge Hamburg, "some new information has just come to my attention that is material to the case and of critical importance to the innocence or guilt of my client. I petition the court to enter new evidence and call a new witness."

"Objection," said Manzo, rising to his feet.

Judge Hamburg banged her gavel. "This is highly irregular, Counsel." She leaned over the bench. "I hope you know what the hell you're doing, Mandy," she said in a stern voice. "Objection overruled." She told Manzo to sit down.

"I enter the following as exhibit number 401," Ms. Greene said. She turned to the homicide detective, whom she had called back to the witness stand. "Could you please tell us what this is?"

"It's a wallet," the detective said.

"Whose wallet is it?" asked Ms. Greene.

"It belonged to the victim."

"I enter the following as exhibit number 402. Could you please tell us what it is?" Ms. Greene said.

"It's a business card."

"Whose business card?"

The detective peered over his glasses to look at it and his eyes widened. "It belongs to Prosecutor Manzo."

"Where did you find it?" asked Ms. Greene.

"In the victim's wallet," the detective said.

A buzz swept through the courtroom. "Objection, Your Honor!" roared Manzo.

"Overruled," Judge Hamburg said severely.

"I enter as exhibit number 403 the following," Ms. Greene said, waving a pile of papers, her normally soft voice assuming a stentorian timbre. "Could you tell us what these are?"

They were hotel bills from the New York Marriott at Brooklyn Bridge. The bills had been issued once a week for the previous nine weeks. The last one was dated November 5—four days before the killing.

"Can you tell us whose name is on the bill?" asked Ms. Greene.

The detective squinted. "Why, it's Prosecutor Manzo."

The prosecutor leapt to his feet again. "Your Honor, I don't see what this has to do with this murder trial."

The judge glared first at Manzo, then Ms. Greene. "This better be good."

"Your Honor, I'd like to call the last witness, Mr. Carl Thuringer," said the lawyer.

A tall man in a dark suit rose and walked toward the witness stand. He had shown up at the trial a few days earlier and stood at the back of the courtroom. He had sought out Mandy Greene during recess, Adam remembered, and spoken to her at length. The bailiff swore him in.

"Mr. Thuringer, can you tell us what you do for a living?" asked Ms. Greene.

"I'm a front desk clerk at the New York Marriott at Brooklyn Bridge."

"Do you recognize anyone in this courtroom?" Ms. Greene asked.

Thuringer looked around and nodded. He pointed to Manzo. "That man. He used to stay at our hotel once a week."

"Do you recognize this woman?" asked Ms. Greene, showing the hotel clerk a photograph of Rebecca Goddard.

"Of course," Thuringer said. "She registered as Mrs. Manzo."

The courtroom spectators gasped.

"Thank you, Mr. Thuringer. That will be all."

Greene turned to face the jury. "Ladies and gentlemen, I am sad to report that my client's wife—the victim—was having an affair. I'm even sadder to report"—and here she jabbed her arm at Prosecutor Manzo—"that her paramour was my colleague." She turned to the judge. "I motion for the immediate declaration of a mistrial and that my client be released at once."

Prosecutor Manzo turned white and his cheeks blazed red. He looked like a bloodstained chef coat. Judge Hamburg hammered her gavel repeatedly, but her efforts to silence the courtroom failed. She summoned both attorneys into her chambers. She emerged a half hour later to announce that she had no choice but to declare a mistrial. Manzo was immediately relieved of his duties as prosecutor.

Adam turned to Greene and lifted her off her feet as he hugged her.

"I'm sorry I waited so long, Adam," she said. "A change of prosecutor would have done us no good. We needed a guaranteed mistrial."

Normally for a crime of this magnitude, the judge would immediately order another trial. But Prosecutor Manzo had so badly botched the first trial and so embarrassed the district attorney, the latter offered the defense a deal. If Adam would plead guilty to involuntary manslaughter, they'd drop the more serious charge of homicide.

Mandy Greene proposed instead an obscure legal option called an Alfred plea. Adam would maintain his innocence, but would acknowledge that there was enough evidence to convict him and therefore would be willing to change his plea to guilty. Eager to be done with the calamitous trial, Judge Hamburg sentenced the onetime celebrity chef to the year he had served in jail already.

Mandy Greene turned out to be considerably more money-conscious than she appeared, presenting Adam with a bill for $250,000, with detailed instructions for wiring the money to an account in the Cayman Islands.

Sylvie went to live with her father, who moved from Paris into Rebecca's apartment. Adam, of course, was denied any contact with the child.

The Silver Bullet closed and another restaurant took its place. Its chef was Tim Dobbins.

As for Adam, technically neither fully exonerated nor proved guilty beyond a shadow of a doubt, he was left jobless and friendless. He had been tried in the court of public opinion the moment the murder accusation went public. That jury declared him guilty.

Claire had listened intently, at times horrified, at times heartbroken.

"Are you Adam Silver?" she asked when the Hermit finally stopped speaking.

"Adam Silver died the day he entered the Alfred plea," the Hermit said.

"So who murdered Rebecca?" Claire asked.

The Hermit shook his head sadly. "I guess you never read to the end of the notebook."

22

you could say we're both victims

The Hermit walked to the bookshelf and pulled out the infamous black binder. "You of all people, Claire," he said. "What sort of editor judges a book before she's read the last page?" His voice was gentle, ironic, playfully mocking. It came the closest Claire would ever hear to a reproach.

He placed the notebook on her lap and went outside to chop wood.

Claire started turning the pages. She thumbed past reviews of the restaurant from a more prosperous time. She thumbed past the articles chronicling the Hermit's arrest and trial.

And there it was at the very end of the notebook: a letter in a plastic sleeve. It was written by hand in the florid script French high schoolers use when they want to show off their penmanship. The return address—45 West End Avenue,

Apartment 5F, New York City—sounded familiar. The letter was dated April 12, 2007.

Claire had been so angry that morning, she hadn't even seen it. Here's what the letter said:

> *Dear Adam,*
>
> *You'll probably be as surprised to read this letter as I am to be writing it. I don't even know if you remember me—the little girl you used to bake gingerbread cookies with in an apartment on West End Avenue. I have enclosed a photograph to refresh your memory.*

Claire looked at the photo clipped to the letter. It had been taken at Adam's restaurant. A little girl sat on his shoulders and a tall woman stood next to him: Julia Child.

> *I have just learned who murdered my mother—your wife—Rebecca. You're in for the shock of your life.*
>
> *I'm not sure how much my mother told you about her first husband, Simon. My father was a musician—a jazz pianist in a trio from Paris. After my mother's death, he and my grandmother moved into our apartment. Simon tried to be a good father, but he wasn't really cut out for parenting. He would come home between gigs, but he never stayed for long. It was my grandmother who raised me.*
>
> *Simon had a drinking problem—that's one of the reasons Mom left him. After her death, he became an alcoholic. He passed away a few weeks ago—not surprisingly of cirrhosis of the liver. Toward the end, I spent a lot of time by his bedside. He wasn't much of a father, like I said, but he was my only surviving parent.*
>
> *The night before he died, he started ranting in his sleep. "I didn't mean to kill her," he said. He said it over and over.*

"Kill whom, Dad?" I asked. I thought he was halluci-
nating.

He opened his eyes and looked at me. "I didn't mean to
kill Rebecca."

"What do you mean, Dad?" I felt like the floor dropped
out from under me.

He slumped back in bed and passed away the next day
without regaining consciousness.

I told my grandmother Simon's last words. She seemed
to age ten years in ten minutes. "Oh, Mon Dieu, non,"
she cried. "Ce n'est pas possible." After we both calmed
down, we pieced together the story.

My father and grandfather had a troubled relationship.
Papi, as I called him, was the fourth-generation owner of a
brewery outside Paris. Naturally, he wanted my father—
his only child—to go into the business. Simon disappointed
him twice—first by becoming a musician and second by
marrying an American. Well, the second disappointment
had a silver lining: Over time my grandfather came to love
Rebecca as he would his own daughter. When my parents
divorced, my grandfather blamed my father. They often
exchanged harsh words. A short time before the murder, my
grandfather swore that when he and my grandmother died,
his entire estate would go to Rebecca.

Among my father's affairs was a battered metal file
box. It contained his papers—songs he had written, newspaper articles about the ensemble, and a few faded photos of
Rebecca. At the bottom of the box, in a velvet bag, were a
shirt and a pair of cotton gloves yellowed with age.

It took us a few minutes to realize that the spattering of
brown spots on the shirt was actually dried blood. Apparently, he wore it the night he bludgeoned my mother.

As for the gloves, according to my grandmother, from
the moment my father started playing the piano as a boy, he

wore cotton gloves to protect his fingers. It always puzzled her why he stopped wearing the gloves the day my mother was killed.

Why he kept these items, I can't say. Perhaps someday he intended to confess. Was the murder premeditated? Was Simon drunk or did he lose control during an argument? I'm afraid we'll never know.

As you can imagine, I was brought up to despise you. I never fully succeeded. I couldn't forget your many kindnesses: how you'd walk me to and from school. How you came home with that cocker spaniel puppy one day. (Remember how I named her Toto?) How we'd make gingerbread people together, rolling the dough with a rolling pin that seemed almost as big as I was.

All this was hard on me, of course, but I can see how it was even harder on you. I guess you could say we're both victims.

Well, I'm all grown up now—a student at Emerson College in Boston. My grandmother helped me track you down through your lawyer. I'll certainly understand if you don't want to see me. If you do, well, we have a lot of catching up to do. You always had a big heart, Adam. I'm hoping you still do and that you can find it in that heart to want to see me.

With love,
Sylvie

So that was it. A false arrest. A life ruined. Claire wiped her eyes, for she had wept while reading the letter.

So that was it. An innocent man tried and condemned for a murder he didn't commit.

But if it hadn't happened, I wouldn't have met the Hermit. The thought flashed through Claire's mind before she could stop it. It made her feel selfish and guilty, but she also felt oddly grateful.

242

She went outside to face the full force of the Hermit's wrath. He had every right to be angry. By all rights, he should send her away with no further conversation.

"Oh, Adam," she said. "I had no idea."

The Hermit sank the ax in the tree stump and looked at her. *Why didn't you just ask me?* he thought, but he didn't say it out loud.

"I'm so sorry," Claire said. "For what I did. For everything that has happened to you. Can you find it in your heart to forgive me."

I let one person into my world in the last fifteen years, the Hermit thought. *And that person turned on me at the first sign of trouble.*

He looked at Claire and said nothing.

"How could I have doubted your innocence—even for a second?" Claire said.

Would you have believed me if I told you what really happened? the Hermit wondered. He looked at Claire, but doubted it.

Claire wiped her eyes on her sleeve for again she had begun to weep. "How can I ever possibly make it up to you?"

The Hermit thought of the food gifts she had cooked for him, of the dinners at the Feinblat cottage. How she opened her home to a vagabond and how she accepted him for who he was.

He put a finger to her lips to shush her. "You already have," he said.

What Claire did next came as naturally as breathing. She reached her arms around him and gave the Hermit a hug. And somewhere, deep within that big bear barrel of a chest, she thought she heard a sob.

23

the hermit is getting a haircut

O uch," said the Hermit.

"Shush," said Molly. "Don't move."

"I think I found a pinecone," said Annabel.

They were seated on the Feinblat deck—the Hermit on a stool in the center; Claire, Sheila, and Annabel gathered around him. Molly stood behind him, comb and scissors in her hand.

Not that Molly knew much about hairstyling, but with all the strange things she had done to her own hair over the years, the task of cutting the Hermit's fell to her. If anyone could hack through his thick mane, it would be Molly. Focused on this formidable task, for once she forgot her anger. The chardonnay flowed (Concord grape juice for Annabel), and the four women were having the time of their lives.

One person was not having the time of his life. As he

watched the hanks of thick gnarled gray hair fall away, the Hermit felt like a knight being stripped of his armor.

"Maybe it's not so terrible to be stripped of your armor," Claire said. "Wilhelm Reich"—now a household name among the assembled party—"spent a lifetime helping people shed their armor: the musculature armor in their bodies, the psychic armor in their minds."

"Ouch," said the Hermit.

"Sit still," said Molly.

"What on earth is going on?" asked Elliott, who had wandered onto the deck.

The four women replied in unison: "The Hermit is getting a haircut."

But even the Hermit had to laugh when Annabel picked up a hank of hair to which she had surreptitiously attached a small pinecone.

It was a warm, luminescent day—the sort that comes to Martha's Vineyard after a May thunderstorm. A gentle breeze blew snippets of hair toward the harbor. By now the Hermit's shoulders and the nape of his neck were visible. Sheila whistled a catcall. Molly stood back to admire her work before attacking the beard.

As for Claire, the book editor found herself at an uncharacteristic loss for words. *Well I'll be damned*, she thought. *He's a hunk.*

The Hermit's rehabilitation proceeded slowly but steadily. His shirts no longer had holes, and he had graduated from flannel. Claire had reacquainted him with the concept that people wear different fabrics in different seasons: wool in the winter; linen in the summer; cotton in spring and fall. His pants were jeans—he would wear jeans to the end of his days—but this pair had no patches.

Claire had insisted they make a shopping expedition to Vineyard Haven.

"François Girbaud or Ralph Lauren Polo?" she asked, holding up what looked to the Hermit to be identical pairs of jeans.

He gave her the most pitifully helpless look a man could muster.

"Polo it is," said Claire, and four pairs of crisp new jeans replaced the patched pants in his wardrobe.

Updating the Hermit's house proved more challenging. Claire had issued an ultimatum with regards to the animal skulls in the yard.

"Me or the bones," she said, and she wiggled her hips provocatively. "After all these years of celibacy," she said, "I imagine you prefer the former."

The Hermit nodded, for he had grown to crave the touch of this woman. So he set about digging a deep hole in the woods, where the animal bones were laid to rest.

"One small step for man," Claire observed.

Encouraged by the progress in the yard, Claire enlisted the help of Molly and Wrench. (The latter was back on the island, although according to Molly, they were now just friends.) Elliott got into the spirit and agreed to do something he, like most intellectuals, had religiously eschewed since college: manual labor. Nate and Annabel insisted on doing their part (once Sheila had doused them with Deet), and even Patrick from the Chappy ferry offered to help.

Wrench pitched in with characteristic zeal, distributing axes, shovels, picks, rakes, and a chain saw. Thus armed, the band converged on the property. As it turned out, the narrow path through the woods behind the cemetery had once been a driveway. Three days of brush cutting made it passable for a motor vehicle. Elliott winced as Patrick hitched an old trailer to the rear bumper of his Jaguar Vanden Plas.

It took six trips to the Edgartown dump to clear the Hermit's property. The crew piled washing machines, refrigerators, sprung furniture, and rotting mattresses into the trailer. Patrick found an antique car collector in Oak Bluffs to buy the '54 Dodge and the old Woody panel truck. An appliance dealer offered them a hundred dollars for the coal-burning stove. Wrench, who worked hard but said little during the proceedings, asked the Hermit if the battered BMW might be reserved for him.

A biker in a Beemer? That was the last straw. Molly didn't even bother to roll her eyes.

Patrick, who, like most male Martha's Vineyarders, seemed to know more than a little about construction, condemned the collapsed porch and dangling entryway as irreparable. The crew donned heavy work gloves and pulled the structures apart, piling the shingles and beams into the trailer. This was easier than it sounds, for the wood was so rotted, it shredded like cotton candy. The rest of the house proved surprisingly solid, although the weathered trim desperately needed a paint job.

The third weekend, Wrench made two important discoveries. The first was an underground propane tank similar to the one at the Feinblat cottage, buried alongside the Hermit's newly cleared driveway. He scraped away the dirt and found a copper line that ran to the Hermit's house. With a little fiddling and a visit by the Vineyard Propane tanker truck, he was able to light the burner on the ancient water heater in the basement. For the first time since he moved into the farmhouse, the Hermit had hot water indoors.

The second discovery involved an electrical panel that had been hidden from view by the collapsed porch. It was an old panel, to be sure, and it took some patient rummaging through the bins at the back of Edgartown Hardware to find old-fashioned mica-fronted screw-in fuses that would fit it.

Meanwhile, Claire did some forensic accounting and discovered that Aunt Tilly had once opened an account with the NSTAR electric company. She changed the account holder's name and told the Hermit how much cash to withdraw from his Edgartown Bank account to restart service. Wrench plugged in an old pole lamp he had unearthed among the rubbish. The friends gathered round and held their breath, as the Hermit—with no small reluctance, it must be said—flipped the switch. For the first time, a lightbulb glowed in the Hermit's living room.

The return of electricity brought three new improvements. The first was a pump, which enabled water tanks to be filled and toilets to be flushed. The Hermit now had indoor plumbing.

The second was a telephone, which Claire insisted was necessary for her to keep in touch with Molly, Sheila, Ely, and the staff at Apogee. So for the first time ever, a ringing phone and a person conversing on it shattered the silence of the Hermit's lair.

Electricity and a working phone line enabled Claire to install the third of the home improvements: a computer. She could now work from the Hermit's house and manage her manuscripts online. As for the Hermit, he avoided it like the plague.

Indoor plumbing? Hot running water? Electricity? Computer and phone?

What more could a woman desire?

As it turned out, not much.

One morning, a robe and a nightgown appeared on hangers in the Hermit's newly organized bedroom closet. Then sweatshirts, jeans, and some women's underwear turned up in his now tidy drawers. The Reich manuscript found a new home—on the claw-foot table in the living room. A new Bose radio was plugged in and the sweet, sad ballads of Norah Jones echoed through the Hermit's house.

It wasn't a conscious or reasoned decision, and it certainly wasn't planned. They didn't so much start living together—they grew together, like two seedlings that had fallen side by side on a patch of Chappaquiddick soil. Claire spent one night at the Hermit's, then another, then a weekend.

And before he knew it, the newly plumbed, efficiently heated, fully electrified, and radically spruced-up Hermit's lair became Claire Doheney's home, too.

Claire's divorce from Harrison came through at the end of August. Barnard College terminated his contract on the grounds that over the last decade, he had sexually harassed more than two dozen of his students. Without a steady source of income, Casanova did what many men of his character would have done: He sued Claire for alimony. The newest full-time resident of Chappaquiddick had no stomach for a protracted legal battle. Happily, the judge threw the case out of court.

When Columbus Day weekend rolled around, passengers waiting for the Chappy ferry on a busy Sunday were astonished to find the *On Time II* out of service. White lace, white streamers, and white roses festooned the boat's wheelhouse and side rails. Elliott, Sheila, Annabel, and Nate had gathered on board. So had Mary, Molly, and Wrench. Dr. Gupta had taken the bus from Manhattan to Woods Hole, where Ely picked her up and brought her across on the Steamship Authority ferry.

Patrick piloted the boat to the middle of the harbor. The Hermit produced a diamond ring that once belonged to Aunt Tilly. Claire stood tall and proud in the white dress she and Molly had picked out at Midnight Farm in Vineyard Haven.

"She chased him until he caught her," Sheila wryly remarked.

Patrick turned to face the assembled crowd and performed one of the lesser-exercised privileges of a sea captain.

Claire and the Hermit—battered survivors of previous marriages—did something that each had vowed never to do again. They asked Patrick Riordan, the ferry captain turned justice of the peace for the occasion, to join them in holy matrimony.

As gentle waves rocked the Chappy ferry in the middle of Edgartown Harbor, Patrick asked Claire and the Hermit the same simple time-honored question.

Each replied in a firm voice: "I do."

24

happily ever after

I wish I could tell you that Claire and the Hermit lived happily ever after. (Not that anyone lives forever.) I wish I could say they lived happily for a long time.

What I can tell you is that for the time they were together, they were happier than either—a cancer survivor and a man wrongfully accused and imprisoned—would ever have dared to dream possible.

So what did it take to make this the happiest couple on Chappaquiddick? Exotic trips? Fashionable parties? Fancy meals at glamorous restaurants in the company of the Martha's Vineyard jet set?

The truth is they were happiest doing what they had done before Claire's bicycle accident brought them together. The Hermit continued to hunt and fish in Chappaquiddick's woods and waterways. Claire continued to fuss over her authors'

manuscripts, polishing words into phrases, building paragraphs into chapters into eloquent books. The Hermit told Claire she was the sexiest double mastectomy in Dukes County, and on moonless nights, she almost believed him.

Their exotic excursions amounted to nothing more than trips to Cronig's Market—or maybe a film at the Edgartown Movie Theater—followed by peppermint ice cream at Scoops. Their meals they cooked themselves—always based on pristine ingredients they gathered or grew—and often enjoyed by the soft glow of a whale-oil lamp. To be sure, the meticulous Hermit found Claire's impetuous cooking style a bit messy sometimes. But he preferred to tidy up after her on the sly rather than to ask her to reform her ways in the kitchen.

They continued their long walks around the island; only now they took them together. The Hermit explained to Claire how he had driven up from New York in the one possession he had left after he had paid his formidable legal expenses and the restaurant's staff and vendors—his BMW convertible. How he arrived at night, under the cover of darkness as it were, and how, thanks to the peanut butter jars left by the farmhouse's previous owner, he hardly had to leave the house for six months.

"There's one thing I don't understand," Claire said. "Why did you keep all those newspaper stories in the loose-leaf binder?"

The Hermit thought about it for a while. "I guess as a reminder that even the best streak of luck can run out. And as your friend Cicero would say, that happiness hangs by a thread."

Claire confessed to following the Hermit around Edgartown after their first dinner at the Feinblat cottage. She told him how difficult it had been for her to trust him after Harrison.

"I can't say I blame you," the Hermit said. "What I want to know is how you had the guts to invite someone who looked as wild and unkempt as I did into your home?"

Claire gave him a mischievous look. "My years as an editor have taught me one thing: Never judge a book by its cover."

Their routine was enlivened by visitors—Sheila and Elliott, Annabel and Nate, Molly and her latest boyfriend, Ely of course, and a new member of the extended family, Patrick the ferryman. Their door was always open. Besides, the Hermit had long since forgotten where he had put the key.

Elliott found in the Hermit a fine mind and interlocutor with whom he could discuss his latest book or philosophical premise.

Nate found in the Hermit a teacher for the one activity at which his famous, otherwise overachieving father was hopelessly inept: fishing.

Annabel found in the Hermit a partner for her latest good work: a Martha's Vineyard literacy drive. The little girl convinced him to contribute the bulk of the books in his library to the effort. Of course, with the eighty-plus cartons of books Claire brought to the marriage, there were plenty to go around.

Ely and the Hermit discussed history and psychology. Patrick just liked hanging around.

Even Wrench showed up from time to time, looking for something to fix.

Claire and Sheila resumed their girls' night out conversations on the Hermit's back porch, only now they sipped not chardonnay, but sarsaparilla.

"How long have you had that cough?" Sheila asked Claire one evening.

Claire put her finger to her lips, then pointed to a magnificent full moon rising over Cape Poge Bay.

Molly came to visit with a new boyfriend in tow.

"Hi, Mom," she said, giving Claire and the Hermit a hug. From a canvas tote bag, she produced a bouquet of roses for her mother.

Claire looked at her dumbstruck.

The boyfriend, who played guitar in a self-styled punk-rap band, went by the name of Strum. His long black hair came halfway down the back of his black jean jacket. A black T-shirt over black jeans and black boots completed the uniform. He had inch-and-a-half-long fingernails on his right hand—the better, he said, to strum his guitar. From the little Claire and the Hermit heard, Strum did not so much play the instrument as subject it to cruel and unusual punishment.

"How long have you had that cough?" Molly asked her mother. Was Claire crazy, or was the habitual sarcasm in Molly's voice tempered by a tinge of concern?

Strum had many annoying habits, not the least of which was calling everyone—from Molly to Claire to the Hermit—"man." He set up his boom box and played raucous music at full blast. His hands pounded percussively on every noise-making surface and a stream of obscene lyrics issued from his mouth.

Claire politely asked him to turn the music down—she was trying to edit.

He kept up with his dissonant singing about "pussy and poontang" and "bitches and hoes."

The Hermit asked him kindly to refrain from singing obscenities in the presence of women. Even Molly tried to shush him.

"Screw me, screw you," Strum sang to Molly, trying out the refrain for a new song by way of a response.

The last great tempest to roar through Martha's Vineyard was Hurricane Bob in 1991. The wind tore barns off their foundations and hurled thirty-foot catboats through the air as though they were walnut shells. The angry seas broke through the beach at Norton's Point, turning Chappaquiddick from a peninsula into an island.

Had Strum looked at the Hermit that moment, he would have seen the fury of gathering storm clouds and anger rising like the tidal wave that completely submerged the western third of the island.

Unfortunately for Strum, he did not.

The Hermit grabbed Strum's ear with the force of a Category 5 hurricane wind. With the other hand, he scooped up the musician's boom box, guitar, and backpack. He marched the startled guitarist to the end of the driveway and flung his arm at the long dirt lane.

"Don't come back until you learn some manners," the Hermit said through clenched teeth.

Molly mouthed the words *thank you* to the Hermit. She had never seen a man stand up for something as old-fashioned as a woman's honor.

An hour later, they heard a timid knock at the door. With ashen face and trembling hands, Strum apologized to Molly. He apologized to Claire, whom for the rest of the weekend he addressed as Ms. Doheney. He didn't know quite what to call the Hermit, so he gave his host wide berth. And he didn't hum, sing, strum, or utter so much as a peep for the rest of his stay.

Claire and the Hermit drove Molly and Strum to the ferry. Claire coughed a good-bye to Molly and gave Strum a mischievous hug.

"What are we going to do about that cough, Claire?" the Hermit asked as they rode back.

"It's nothing," said Claire.

But the cough got worse.

"Shouldn't we go see Dr. Gupta?" asked the Hermit a few days later. Not that he relished returning to New York—the scene of so much misfortune for him—but Claire's well-being mattered more to the Hermit than anything else in his life.

"It's nothing," said Claire. She did not tell the Hermit she had met with Dr. Gupta a few weeks earlier when she went to New York to finalize some legal details remaining from the divorce.

"I'm afraid I have some bad news," Dr. Gupta said after examining the X-rays. "The cancer has returned. It has metastasized in your ribs and lungs."

Claire exhaled slowly. "Do I have any options?"

Dr. Gupta came around from behind her desk. She stood on her box and gave Claire a hug. "We could put you on another course of chemotherapy," said Dr. Gupta. "Of course, it would need to be very aggressive."

"What are the odds it would work?" Claire asked.

"I'll be honest with you," said Dr. Gupta, looking down at her orthopedic shoes. "It's a long shot."

"If you don't mind," Claire said, "I'd rather die with hair on my head."

The cough persisted. It was now joined by a pain in Claire's chest that even the stoic Irish Catholic couldn't completely hide. The Hermit had taken over most of the cooking, but Claire didn't have much appetite. She curtailed her long walks with the Hermit in the face of her growing shortness of breath.

The Hermit acquired a new walking partner: Molly. The girl—sans boyfriend these days—took the bus up from New York every weekend. On one visit, in addition to what had become customary flowers for Claire, she produced a small neatly wrapped package for the Hermit. The girl fidgeted as the Hermit opened the box and pulled out a shiny white fishing lure with an orange tip and treble fishhooks. "It's a Spofford's Ballistic Missile," Molly said. "Patrick the ferry guy helped me pick it out. It's supposed to be really good for bluefish."

The Hermit thanked her with his customary formality, but Claire could see how deeply the gesture moved him. She smiled at the obvious symbolism. Could her diffident daughter actually be fishing for the Hermit's affection? Could the erstwhile misanthrope actually have taken the bait?

The next time Molly came, she found a long slender case on the bed of what had come to be regarded as her bedroom. It contained a custom-rigged Ron Arra fishing rod with Molly's name engraved on the handle. The Hermit took Molly to Wasque Point, where he initiated her in the art of surfcasting. He didn't speak much, and Molly was grateful for his silence. Adults, it seemed, were always trying too hard to draw her out of her shell. But when Molly came home after catching her first bluefish, she fairly bounced off the walls with excitement.

Come Sunday afternoon, when Molly went to kiss her mother good-bye, Claire noticed the girl had replaced some of the safety pins in her ears with a lure from the Hermit's tackle box.

Ely drove down from Maine to wrap up the Reich biography. It was a dramatic denouement to a turbulent life, and Ely wanted Claire's help to get it right.

There's an old saying in legal circles: Only a fool would hire himself as his lawyer. Reich's trial for contempt for the FDA injunction began on May 3, 1956. The doctor defended himself. In this his legal skills did not measure up to his competence in psychotherapy. It took the jury all of fifteen minutes to come to a verdict: guilty. When Judge George Sweeney delivered the sentence, he was convinced that an unrepentant swindler stood before him. The severity of the sentence surprised even the prosecutor: two years in federal prison and a ten-thousand-dollar fine. The Supreme Court refused to hear the appeal.

The remaining orgone energy accumulators at Orgonon and in New York were destroyed. Six *tons* of Reich's books were burned in an incinerator in Manhattan's Meatpacking District. Sadly, Reich was no stranger to book burning. After all, he had lived in Nazi Germany prior to immigrating to the United States.

On March 12, 1957, handcuffs were snapped on the one-time disciple of Freud and wunderkind of the Viennese psychoanalytic community. He was taken to a federal penitentiary in Danbury, Connecticut, then transferred to a prison in Lewisburg, Pennsylvania.

In late October, Reich fell ill with chest pains. He said nothing to the prison doctor, for in a few days, he was scheduled for a parole hearing. On November 3, he failed to show up at roll call. The prison officials found him lying on his bed, fully clothed except for his shoes. Earlier that morning, Wilhelm Reich died in his sleep of what the medical examiner diagnosed in his report as myocardial insufficiency with sudden heart failure.

Ely put it in poignant plain English: The sixty-year-old Wilhelm Reich had died of a broken heart.

Later that day, when Claire lay down to rest, Ely took the Hermit aside on the porch.

"She's dying," he said. "I know I'm stating the obvious—it must be painful for you to acknowledge."

The Hermit swallowed.

"Dr. Reich did a lot of work with cancer," Ely said. "He believed you could heal it with an orgone energy accumulator."

The Hermit swallowed again. "So where do we get an orgone accumulator?" he asked.

"You can't," said Ely. "The FDA outlawed it."

The Hermit looked crestfallen.

"But there's no reason we can't build one," Ely said, and the men sprang into action. Fifteen minutes later, they drove Ely's Volkswagen onto the ferry, bound for Cottle's lumber in Edgartown.

By the time Ely and the Hermit had tied all the wood, sheet metal, and spun glass insulation onto the roof, you could barely see the car. The vehicle looked so precarious, Patrick refused to allow any other cars on the ferry when he took them across. Or maybe he was just trying to get them home faster.

Somehow, Wrench had caught wind of the accumulator project, and was waiting impatiently at the farmhouse with his toolbox when the Hermit and Ely returned. The men set up sawhorses, measured and cut boards, unrolled and snipped insulation, twisted sheet metal, pounded nails, and screwed in finishing screws. If Claire wondered about the strange noises emanating from the backyard of the farmhouse—buzz saws, electric drills, pneumatic hammers—she was too weak to ask.

That evening, under Ely's supervision, Claire sat in the newly constructed accumulator for an hour—a regimen she followed daily for the next several weeks.

It was here that the miracle happened. By the end of the first week, her chest pains disappeared. By the end of the second week, her cough had completely subsided. By the third week, her strength had returned enough for Claire to resume her daily walks with the Hermit.

Again, Ely urged Claire to try some of his bioenergetic exercises, and this time she agreed. The farmhouse on Cape Poge Bay resounded with strange kicking noises and screams and thumps.

Wrench—now something of a bioenergetic disciple himself—checked in from time to time to make sure Claire did the exercises correctly.

Strum would have felt right at home, thought Molly, who was on the island for one of her visits. But the dissonant guitarist had decided to enroll in the Juilliard School. It seems he had taken up a more peaceable instrument: Strum now plucked a lute.

Life gradually got back to normal, and it began to seem like happily ever after might not be just a fairy tale after all.

25

---

hoping for a meal of fish guts

They scattered her ashes from the back of the ferry over Edgartown Harbor.

The seagulls swooped in low, hoping for a meal of fish guts.

Patrick had draped the side rails and wheelhouse of the *On Time II* with black crepe paper. They put the second ferry into service even though it was low season, so the first boat could be used for the memorial service.

Elliott and Sheila drove up from New York with Annabel. Nate was away on a field trip. Dr. Gupta rode in the Jaguar in his place. She didn't take up much space. Molly arrived on the back of Wrench's Harley Fat Boy. Ely, wearing his trademark rumpled suit and Birkenstocks, rode down from Rangeley, stopping in Boston to pick up Mary Doheney and Claire's sisters. His bushy eyebrows and bottlebrush mustache drooped in mourning for the editor and friend he had lost.

Beidermann from Apogee Publishing did not come. Out-of-state bereavement expenses were no longer covered by the editorial travel budget. Besides, he had been to Chappaquiddick to meet with Claire a few weeks earlier.

The islanders came, too, and the Hermit was amazed at how many local lives Claire seemed to have touched in the brief years she had lived on Martha's Vineyard. Rhonda, Claire's yoga teacher, arrived with four women from her yoga class. The bartender from Alchemy came, as did the owner of Espresso Love. Eight women from the Breast Cancer Survivors Support Group showed up.

The ninth woman, Marge, was away in Boston for the weekend with her husband. The final round of reconstructive surgery left her with two cancer-free breasts worthy of a Victoria's Secret catalog. She and the Sergeant decided to celebrate with a romantic weekend at the Mandarin Oriental Hotel.

Patrick piloted the ferry turned funeral barge, and all but one of the other ferry captains came on board to pay their last respects. That captain was driving the other boat. He issued a mournful wail from its foghorn. A handful of local fishermen turned up to show solidarity with the Hermit, whom they had come to regard as one of their own. Ely helped Dr. Gupta stand on one of the passenger benches so she could participate in the ceremony.

Like Aunt Tilly, Claire had insisted on being cremated. "I've taken up enough space on this planet," she said. These final dispositions proved more complicated than you might imagine. The Hermit had to pay for the funeral parlor to send a hearse over from Hyannis. He followed silently as they took Claire's body on the Chappy ferry, then to Vineyard Haven, then up the Steamship Authority ferry ramp onto a freight boat for the trip back to Cape Cod.

The ashes came back two days later in a brass urn with Claire's name engraved on a plaque on the front. The sight of it left the Hermit with a pit in his stomach. Maybe it was similar to the pit Claire described when she was undergoing chemotherapy.

Elliott led the service. "A little bird has flown away from us," he said. "Her name was Claire Doheney."

Sheila sobbed loudly.

"There are three kinds of people in this world," Elliott continued. "Those who make it worse; those who leave it about the same as they found it; and those who make it better. The first often go into politics," said Elliott, and here everyone laughed. "The second, well, they're ordinary folks like you and me. The third—they're the rare, gifted, singular people who make the world a truly better place for all of us.

"Claire made the world better in many ways," Elliott said.

"As a daughter and sister." Here he turned to Mary and to Claire's siblings, Deirdre and Megan.

"As a mother." Here he looked at Molly.

"As a wife." Here he turned to face the Hermit.

"And as a friend." Here he turned to Sheila and Annabel and struggled to hold back his own tears.

"As an editor, she made the world a better place in many ways, too, not least of which was by enabling an army of starving writers to realize the dream of being published." Here he turned to Ely, whose mustache rose in a smile.

"A quick survey of her books reflects the incredible breadth of her literary passions. Ancient Rome. Musical Venice. Fin de siècle Paris. And now, Freudian Vienna and New York. Praise came to her openly and abundantly, but to the end, she always deflected the spotlight onto her authors."

Then Elliott asked if anyone else wanted to say a few words. He had spoken so eloquently, no one else stepped forward. The Hermit felt that he should make some final remark, but his mind and mouth felt paralyzed. He watched the ashes settle on the water. Tears rolled silently down his cheeks. Molly reached for his hand.

They went back to the Feinblat cottage for the wake or shivah or whatever you call a house in mourning for a dead Catholic who had married a lapsed Jew. The out-of-towners were invited to stay through the weekend. And gradually, what began in sadness for a funeral became a celebration of Claire's life.

There was even a moment of levity on the third morning, when everyone had gone to Edgartown for breakfast. The housekeeper was tidying Dr. Gupta's room and what did she find next to the bed? As she told Sheila later that day, clucking her tongue, "Ely Samuelson's Birkenstocks, that's what."

Claire had conducted her final weeks with the same purposeful dignity with which she had lived her life.

First, she summoned Beidermann. Claire wanted to make sure the Reich book would be published and promoted in a manner worthy of a Men of Action title. She also announced a new acquisition—*In Rembrandt's Kitchen*—a domestic biography of the Dutch master to be written by an author Claire had met on Martha's Vineyard. It, too, was to be properly published and promoted, she told Beidermann—time sheets and costs be damned.

Next, she summoned Harrison—unpleasant as it was for Claire and the Hermit—to discuss Molly's future. "She's your daughter as well as mine," said Claire. "I promise, if you don't provide properly for her, I'll come back to haunt you for the rest of your days."

"You're joking, right?" Harrison asked nervously. Chappaquiddick gave him the creeps.

At that very moment, another visitor at the far end of the house—the soon-to-be-famous biographer of Wilhelm Reich—started his daily bioenergetic exercises. A bloodcurdling scream and a series of loud thumps emanated from the Hermit's guest room.

The hair on Harrison's neatly coiffed head stood on end. He promised to do whatever Claire asked.

The third visitor did not come specifically to see Claire, although she had worked hard to facilitate the meeting. The Hermit paced the farmhouse nervously for days prior to the visit. At Claire's urging, he had finally written to an Emerson College coed named Sylvie.

Molly drove the Hermit to the Steamship Authority ferry terminal in Vineyard Haven to meet his erstwhile stepdaughter—the girl on his shoulders in the photograph at Adam's restaurant. Her pale skin and coal black hair reminded him of Rebecca. Molly dropped them off at the Café Moxie so they could have some time by themselves over lunch. Later, she brought them back to the Chappaquiddick farmhouse for a reprise of Claire's Franco–New England dinner. The Hermit spoke little of the visit, but the following week, Molly and Claire observed a startling new behavior—they actually heard him humming.

As the end approached, Claire summoned the Feinblats to thank them for their lifelong friendship. And for introducing her to Chappaquiddick. She encouraged Annabel to continue her good works helping other people and told Nate to keep his fishing line—and life—unsnarled. She asked Sheila and Elliott to look after Molly—and their strange new friend, the Hermit.

As for Molly, Claire had thought hard and long about what she should say. She had thought about telling Molly how lucky she was to have been born; Claire's first two pregnancies had ended in miscarriage.

But in the end she decided not to. Instead, she distilled what her own life had taught her about motherhood into four simple sentences.

"I love you," she told Molly.

"I trust you," she said.

"Have confidence in yourself, Molly. You can do anything."

She was quiet for a minute; then she added: "And know, whatever you do, I'll be proud of you."

When Molly thought about it many years afterwards—a mother herself by then—she realized that's all a parent really needs to say.

And the Hermit? Well, Claire simply thanked him for his love and for letting her into his world on Chappaquiddick. He sat with her, holding her hand, as her life flickered and faded. Her final words came from an old John Donne poem.

"Adam," she said. "No man is an island."

She looked at him. Then closed her eyes. And Claire Doheney was gone.

epilogue

babies, bottles, and bassinets

A sound arose in the silent sanctuary that had once been the Hermit's lair.

It began as a whimper, grew to a moan, then a sob, a cry, and a howl. It steadily increased in volume and duration from a wail to a full-blown shriek. It echoed off walls and bounced off the ceiling, rattling the kitchen windows. It shattered the calm of the farmhouse like the roar of a fighter jet from Otis Air National Guard Base on nearby Cape Cod breaking the sound barrier.

It was a baby, and it was crying. And by all appearances, it was hungry.

A second sound arose in the Hermit's once quiet lair.

It began as a gurgle, grew to a hiss, and crescendoed in a high-pitched whistle loud enough to curdle your blood.

It came from an old-fashioned teakettle that had been put on a wood-burning cookstove to boil.

A third noise arose outside the Hermit's lair.

It began as a distant rumble, became a low-pitched roar, and ended in a theatrical screech of brakes in the driveway. There was a thump of heavy boots on wooden stairs and across a wooden deck, then the squeak of a spring and the slamming of a screen door.

It was the sound of a Harley-Davidson Fat Boy thundering up the dirt lane, then of its rider climbing the stairs to the Hermit's porch and opening the back door.

A fourth sound came from outside the Hermit's house—this one emanating from another internal combustion engine. It was the quiet hum of a Jaguar and it was followed by the whine of an electric window and the thunk of a car door, then the slapping pitter-patter of rubber on the wooden stairs and deck. The spring squeaked again and the screen door again bounced against its frame.

The hum, whine, and thunk came from Elliott's Vanden Plas, parked next to a BMW, now restored to showroom condition for the Hermit by the rider of the Harley-Davidson. The pitter-patter was produced by Annabel's flip-flops as she bounded up the Hermit's stairs.

A lot had changed since the Hermit had met, married, and lost Claire. This cacophony was part of his new life.

The baby belonged to Molly—a baby girl with Claire's chestnut hair and pale Irish Catholic complexion. Her name was Samantha—already everyone called her Sam—and she was born seven months earlier, shortly before Molly entered medical school.

The baby's father was likely the rider of the Harley-Davidson. It turned out that Molly and Wrench were more than just friends after all. When Wrench learned of his possible paternity, he did about the last thing Molly expected. He stepped forward, insisted on paying child support, and volunteered to help take care of the baby.

It seems that Wrench had picked up a copy of *It's Your Responsibility*—written by a certain Chappaquiddick summer resident named Elliott Feinblat—and had taken the book to heart. Patrick got him a job as deckhand on the Chappy ferry. Wrench read everything he could about childrearing, from Dr. Spock to *What to Expect When You're Expecting*. Not that Wrench aspired to become Molly's husband, at least not yet—both parties had matured enough to realize that neither was sufficiently mature for marriage.

Wrench considered the deckhand job as a paid opportunity to learn about commercial navigation. The owner of the Chappy ferry came to appreciate his mechanical prowess. A jammed clutch cable or broken ramp counterweight chain that once put the ferry out of commission for the better part of a day took the dexterous Wrench less than an hour to repair.

Wrench became the de facto mechanic for a lot of the boats in Edgartown Harbor. Soon he earned enough money to take an apartment over Sandpiper Realty. Every afternoon, after his shift, he would ride his motorcycle to Chappaquiddick to help the Hermit care for the baby.

He was joined in this endeavor by the flip-flop-wearing Annabel, who decided that her social conscience could be better assuaged by helping a clueless widower and bachelor care for an infant than by feeding the homeless. Besides, she reasoned, you could never *really* be sure who was homeless and who wasn't.

Which brings us to the final sound in this familial cacophony: the shriek of the teakettle.

When Molly, four months pregnant, was accepted to Tufts School of Medicine, she went not to her father or Elliott or Wrench for advice. She sought out the Hermit. She started with a litany of her mistakes and her regrets. How sorry she was for hurting her mother; how badly she had screwed up her life. He shushed her with a gesture he had used with Claire: a finger to her lips.

"What would your mother tell you to do?" he asked.

Molly thought about it awhile. "She would have told me I could be anything I wanted to be. She'd have told me to go to medical school *and* have the baby. She'd have told me to figure it out."

Which is precisely what Molly did—with a little help from the Hermit.

The Hermit had spent so little of Aunt Tilly's stipend over the years, his savings more than sufficed to pay for Molly's tuition. Which came in handy, for the girl had severed all ties with her father.

You're growing more like your mother every day, thought the Hermit. Not that he told Molly. After all, a rebel has to keep up appearances.

They agreed that Molly would go to Tufts during the week and come to the Vineyard on the weekends and during the summer. Wrench would contribute in whatever way his heart or wallet inspired him to. And the Hermit, at the age of sixty, would teach himself a new skill. He'd learn to take care of a baby.

The Hermit took the boiling water off the stove and slowly poured it into a pot in which stood a bottle of baby formula. He swirled the bottle around for thirty seconds, then touched it to the inside of his wrist. When he deemed it warm enough, he took the formula bottle in one hand and cradled Samantha in the opposite arm. Within seconds, the squalling subsided. And Samantha gazed at the Hermit with adoring green eyes as she ate.

"Babies, bottles, bassinets," grumbled the Hermit of Chappaquiddick, adding a loud "harrumph" for emphasis. He shook his head with mock irritation.

But no one in the room—not Wrench, not Annabel, not Sheila or Elliott, not Nate who had come for his daily fishing lesson, not Molly who had arrived during the feeding—not one of them in the room bought it for a second.

afterword

T he main characters in this book are fictional, but the places they inhabit and issues they deal with are real.

To the best of my knowledge, there has never been a Hermit of Chappaquiddick. In four hundred years of written history, however, and very likely before, plenty of loners, misfits, recluses, and just plain strange characters have made this island their home. The Hermit's domicile is as fictional as its inhabitant. There are no woods next to the cemetery with a hidden path through it, nor a junkyard or house at the end, so please don't bother looking for them.

I feel obliged to warn you that I've made Chappaquiddick sound a lot more inviting than it really is. The ferry lines are horrendous; the locals are hostile; and the mosquitoes are the size of hummingbirds. (And don't get me started about deer ticks.) The dirt roads will rattle any good sense you may have out of your skull in a matter of minutes. There are no hotels, restaurants, or really much of anything to do here. In short, Chappaquiddick may be a fit place for a Hermit, but it's a terrible place for everyone else.

The book titles *Radiant*; *I, Cicero*; and *Mozart's Wordsmith* are made up, but their contents are based on existing books. Ditto for Claire's Men of Action biography of Wilhelm Reich. As far as I know, no one has yet written a book called *It's Your Responsibility*, but the longer I live, the more I'd like to read it. These titles are up for grabs: use them if you're so inspired, and remember to send me a copy.

Dr. Wilhelm Reich did, indeed, die in a federal penitentiary on November 3, 1957. At the time of his death, most of his writings and books were banned and his orgone accumulator outlawed. Today, his work lives on at the Wilhelm Reich Institute and Museum at Orgonon in Rangeley, Maine. Rangeley is lovely to visit (a lot nicer than Chappaquiddick); while there, you can sit in an orgone energy box and even rent a cabin on the museum grounds. Conferences on Reich's work are held there every summer, and scholarly journals have once again started to issue from Reich's press.

Last but not least . . . as a Chappaquiddick resident, I apologize in advance to my neighbors for any unwanted attention this novel may bring to our island. A portion of the proceeds from the sale of each book will go to the Chappaquiddick Open Space Fund of the Sheriff's Meadow Foundation.

acknowledgments

No man is an island. This novel wouldn't exist without the gracious support of many family members, friends, colleagues, and experts. It gives me great pleasure to thank:

My wife, Barbara, who aids, abets, nurtures, and puts up with me in this and all my ventures. She has a wonderful gift of being able to bring out the best in me, while turning a (mostly) blind eye to the worst.

My assistant, Nancy Loseke, an exacting editor and true friend.

My agents, Jane Dystel and Miriam Goderich of Dystel & Goderich Literary Management, whose expertise and perseverance helped bring this book to life.

My editor at Tor Forge, Robert Gleason (an accomplished novelist in his own right). Tom Doherty, Linda Quinton, Katherine Critchlow, Whitney Ross, Eric C. Meyer, and copy editor Eliani Torres.

Bill Martin, a fellow Tor Forge author, who introduced me to Bob. I met Bill at the home of our Chappaquiddick neighbors and friends Lionel and Vivian Spiro. Lionel also taught me how to catch bay scallops using a peep box. (I'm still wondering why his bucket is always twice as full as mine.)

Fellow writers John Dufresne, Rick Flaste, Cal Fussman, Brian Rochlin, Les Standiford, and Leslie Wells; longtime friends Shirley Drevich, Kathleen Hawley, and Cynthia Kropp; and of course the inimitable Mitchell Kaplan of Books & Books in Miami. All took time to read the manuscript and improve it with their comments. Eileen Nexer, next in command after Barbara, who gave her usual wise counsel and came up with the line "A Novel of Love, Loss, Redemption, and Really Good Food."

Dr. Enrique Davila, Dr. Peter Gillespie, and Dr. Lance Raiffe, who expertly diagnosed the health issues in the story, and my legal team—Jamie Gardner, Peter Gillespie, Bob Luskin, Jeff Zach, and my brother-in-law Andy Lehrman—who kept me honest on the fine points of criminal and civil law.

Hatsy Potter, editor of *Chappaquiddick: That Sometimes Separated But Never Equalled Island*; Paul Schultz and the Trustees of Reservations; and Matthew Stackpole of the Martha's Vineyard Historical Society, who enlightened me on the history of Martha's Vineyard and Chappaquiddick.

Naturalist Russ Cohen and the Polly Hill Arboretum, who introduced me to Chappaquiddick's many edible and medicinal plants.

I first learned of the work of Dr. Wilhelm Reich, bioenergetics, and psychodrama from the late Bob and Ildri Ginn and later from Reich's biographer, Dr. Myron Sharaf.

La Varenne founder Anne Willian and La Varenne chefs Fernand Chambrette and Albert Jorant taught me more than a little about French cuisine and life.

Chappy ferry captain Bob Gilkes graced the cover of this book with his handsome photography.

Last but not least, the next generation of Chappaquiddickers: Betsy, Jake, and Gabriel, and of course, Ella, Mia, and Julian.

bibliography

About Chappaquiddick and Martha's Vineyard

Chappaquiddick: That Sometimes Separated But Never Equalled Island, 2nd ed. Edited by Hatsy Potter. Martha's Vineyard, Massaschusetts: Chappaquiddick Island Association, 2008.

Cohen, Russ. *Wild Plants I Have Known . . . and Eaten.* Illustrated by Stephanie Letendre. Essex, Massachusetts: Essex County Greenbelt Association, 2004.

Horwitz, Tony. *A Voyage Long and Strange.* New York: Henry Holt and Company, 2008.

Potter, Edo. *Pimpneymouse Farm: The Last Farm on Chappaquiddick.* Edgartown, Massachusetts: Vineyard Stories, 2010.

Railton, Arthur R. *The History of Martha's Vineyard.* Beverly, Massachusetts: Commonwealth Editions (published in association with the Martha's Vineyard Historical Society), 2006.

Schneider, Paul. *The Enduring Shore.* New York: Henry Holt and Company, 2000.

Medical and Psychological Studies

Hirshaut, Yashar, M.D., and Peter I. Pressman, M.D. *Breast Cancer: The Complete Guide.* 4th ed. New York: Bantam Dell, 2004.

Man's Right to Know, DVD produced by the Wilhelm Reich Infant Trust, 2002.

Reich, Wilhelm. *The Function of the Orgasm, Character Analysis, Listen, Little Man!,* and other books. New York: Farrar, Straus and Giroux, 1986, 1980, 1974.

Sharaf, Myron. *Fury on Earth.* New York: St. Martin's Press/
Marek, 1983.

Miscellaneous
Haller, James. *The Blue Strawberry Cookbook.* Boston: Harvard
Common Press, 1976.